'I wasn't suggesting you should sleep with me while we're in Paris, Mattie—'

'I told you, I'm not going to Paris with you!' she told him with firm finality.

While, at the same time, her imagination ran amok with visions of Jack Beauchamp and herself, locked languidly together, their naked bodies passionately entwined as they kissed and caressed each other…

'I doubt we would do much sleeping if we were to share a bedroom anywhere, Mattie.'

Jack's murmured comment interrupted her intimate imaginings.

Carole Mortimer was born in England, the youngest of three children. She began writing in 1978, and has now written over 90 books for Harlequin Mills & Boon. Carole has four sons, Matthew, Joshua, Timothy and Peter, and a bearded collie dog called Merlyn. She says, 'I'm in a very happy relationship with Peter senior; we're best friends as well as lovers, which is probably the best recipe for a successful relationship. We live on the Isle of Man.'

Recent titles by the same author:

BRIDE BY BLACKMAIL
AN ENIGMATIC MAN
KEEPING LUKE'S SECRET

IN SEPARATE
BEDROOMS

BY
CAROLE MORTIMER

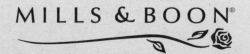

First published in Great Britain 2003
Harlequin Mills & Boon Limited,
Eton House, 18-24 Paradise Road, Richmond, Surrey TW9 1SR

© Carole Mortimer 2003

ISBN 0 263 83323 2

Set in Times Roman 10½ on 12¼ pt.
01-1003-44080

Printed and bound in Spain
by Litografía Rosés, S.A., Barcelona

CHAPTER ONE

'THE man is nothing but a womaniser!' Mattie told her mother, every inch of her slender five-feet-two-inch-frame bristling with emotion, blue eyes sparkling brightly in the delicate beauty of her heart-shaped face. Even her wild mane of tawny-coloured, below shoulder-length hair seemed to spark with the intensity of her indignation.

'Mattie, it sounds to me as if you've made another one of your snap judgements,' her mother admonished lightly as she sat behind her desk. 'And we both know how often they've been wrong in the past,' she added. 'Besides, Mattie,' she continued gently, 'are you sure you aren't just overreacting because after dating Richard for three months last year you found out he was actually engaged to marry someone else?'

In truth, Mattie preferred not to think of the humiliation she had felt when Richard had informed her they couldn't see each other any more because he was getting married the following week!

'Although, from what you've told me about him, this man does sound a little—free with his company,' her mother conceded as Mattie went on looking fretful.

'A *little*?' Mattie repeated disgustedly. 'I told you, the man has four women on the go, Mum. Four!' she echoed incredulously. 'And three of them appear to be married.'

'Then they ought to know better,' her mother dismissed, an older, slightly plumper version of her pretty daughter. 'I'm afraid it's a fact of life that some men seem to think there's safety in numbers!'

Mattie frowned. 'Safety from what?'

'Marriage-minded women, usually.' Her mother smiled wryly.

'What woman in her right mind could possibly want to marry a man like that?' Mattie scorned. 'He's nothing but a greedy pig!'

'Personally, I think he ought to be taken out into the streets and publicly whipped,' drawled a huskily amused—distinctly male!—voice.

Mattie froze where she stood in front of the desk behind which her mother sat working, very reluctant to turn round, her face bright red with embarrassment. She had been totally unaware that their conversation was being listened to—and by a man, of all people!

Her mother felt no such awkwardness, smiling across the room at the man as she stood up to move around her desk. 'Can I help you?'

'Jack Beauchamp,' the man introduced. 'I telephoned you yesterday about the possibility of booking my dog in here next weekend. You suggested I come and have a look round first,' he reminded her.

Mattie's face went pale. *This* man was a potential customer—at least, his dog was!—at her mother's boarding-kennels...?

'I hope I'm not interrupting anything...?' he added with light query. 'You did say I could call in some time on Sunday afternoon.'

Mattie swallowed hard, desperately willing the colour back into her cheeks, knowing she had never felt so mortified—and uncomfortable—in her life.

'Of course, Mr Beauchamp,' her mother replied

smoothly. 'I'll be quite happy to show you round. You have a Bearded Collie, I believe?'

Good old Mum. Mattie smiled affectionately; she never forgot a dog or its breed—although very often the owners were another matter entirely.

'Harry,' Jack Beauchamp confirmed. 'But if you're busy, I'm quite happy for your assistant to show me round…?'

Assistant? Yes, that was probably exactly what she seemed to this man, Mattie conceded. After all, she was dressed in jeans and skimpy blue tee shirt, ideal wear for working in the kennels. In fact, she usually gave her mother a hand on Sundays. It just wasn't what she did the rest of the week…

She drew in a deep breath before turning, her breath catching in her throat as she found herself looking at the most attractive man she had ever set her deep blue eyes on!

Probably aged in his early thirties, tall, and leanly built, his dark hair kept fashionably short, he had the deepest brown eyes Mattie had ever seen. Like liquid chocolate, she decided. Warm.

Caressing. Fathomless. And the rest of his face wasn't bad, either, she conceded grudgingly; lean and tanned, his nose looking as if it might have been broken some years back, his mouth full and smiling, only the stubborn set of the chin belying his relaxed pose in a black tee shirt and dark blue denims.

'I would be happy to show you around, Mr Beauchamp.' She nodded coolly. 'As you say, my mother is rather busy at the moment,' she finished pointedly.

'Ah.' He nodded, those deep brown eyes openly

laughing at her now, at her subtle correction of who she was.

No 'I'm sorry for the mistake.' No polite 'I should have realized, the two of you are very alike.' Just that slightly mocking 'ah'!

'Oh, but—'

'Do please carry on with what you were doing, Mum,' Mattie interrupted firmly, her hackles very definitely up. 'I'm sure Mr Beauchamp and I can manage very well together.'

Her mother shot her a worriedly questioning look. A look Mattie met with an innocent raise of her tawny brows. Her mother probably didn't realize it, but Mattie was in just the mood to deal with the over-confident Mr Beauchamp! Or perhaps, after their recent conversation, about greedy pigs, her mother did realize it, and that was why she was looking so worried...

The boarding-kennels had been going through a hard time in the last year, too many people seeing the opportunity to run their own business from their own home, and jumping on the bandwagon, having no real idea of the hard work involved, the long hours of business, being on call twenty-four hours a day to their furry charges.

But The Woofdorf was, as its name implied, a superior boarding-kennels in Mattie's—biased?—opinion and had been her mother's pride and joy for the last twenty years. A fact Jack Beauchamp—although he didn't realize it—was about to find out.

She gave him a withering look. 'If you would like to follow me, Mr Beauchamp, I will show you our indoor accommodation for our guests.'

'Blow in my ear, and I'll follow you anywhere.'

Mattie turned sharply at these startling words, frowning darkly as she found Jack Beauchamp had taken her literally concerning the instruction 'follow me', and he was now standing so close to her she found herself with her nose almost pressed against the muscled hardness of his chest.

She took an involuntary step backwards before answering him. 'I beg your pardon?' Surely he couldn't really have said what she had thought he had—murmured, really; her mother, smiling after them politely, certainly didn't seem to have heard those provocative words.

Jack Beauchamp's gaze met hers with unblinking innocence. 'I said the weather is very pleasant for this time of year,' he said pleasantly, dark gaze laughingly challenging. In fact, the man seemed to have been inwardly laughing at her since the moment he'd interrupted her conversation with her mother.

And Mattie didn't believe for a moment that he had said what he claimed he had!

'After you, Mr Beauchamp,' she invited stiffly as she pointedly held the door open for him to precede her outside.

'No, after you, Miss Crawford.' He gave a mocking inclination of his dark head.

Mattie was sure it wasn't an accident that, just as she was about to go through the doorway, he decided to go through it too, crushing her back up against the doorframe, the softness of her shapely curves pressed against his body from chest to thigh.

'Sorry,' she muttered as the two of them popped through the doorway together like a cork from a champagne bottle.

'My pleasure,' he drawled, his dark gaze *definitely* mocking now as the two of them stood outside in the spring sunshine.

She would just bet it was, her whole body tingling from the unexpected contact with his, even more convinced as he gave a disarming grin that he had done it on purpose.

'Perhaps if you didn't follow quite so closely, Mr Beauchamp…' she said tersely.

His mouth was still curved into that increasingly infuriating smile. 'I'll try not to, Miss Crawford,' he obeyed as he followed her down the flowered pathway to the indoor kennels. 'You seem slightly familiar,' he murmured quizzically after several seconds. 'Could we possibly have met before?'

Mattie drew in a deep breath. Could he possibly have realized what she really did for a living, how the two of them had in fact met? If he had, then it wasn't going to take too much guesswork on his part to add two and two together and come up with the required four. Nothing for it; for the sake of her mother's business, she would just have to deny all knowledge!

She glanced back to answer him—only to find his gaze very firmly fixed on the graceful sway of her hips as she walked.

Well, really! Didn't the man ever switch from flirtation mode down to coasting? Today, at least, she was the equivalent of a kennel-maid, for goodness' sake!

'Somehow I very much doubt that we move in the same social circles, Mr Beauchamp,' she responded.

'I don't have a social circle, Miss Crawford,' he drawled. 'No, I'm sure I've never met you at a party or anything like that,' he continued slowly, dark eyes narrowed thoughtfully as he now studied the delicate beauty of her face. 'I just have a feeling of—familiarity.' He gave a rueful shrug.

'Well, I can assure you I don't have the same feeling.' Mattie gave a dismissive laugh, long sooty lashes coming down to cover the anger now blazing in her eyes. And he could take that remark however he chose—either they had never met before, or he was so unremarkable that she didn't remember him!

Except that she did...

'This way,' she instructed sharply, unlocking the door that went through to the indoor kennels, a riotous barking beginning as the dogs sensed company. 'All our rooms are carpeted, as well as centrally heated.' She reached down and stroked each of the dogs through wire-netted doors as they passed the rooms. 'There is also a chair for those that prefer it. The basket and bedding is replaced with each new guest, although we appreciate that very often you prefer to bring your pet's own bedding.' She launched automatically into professional dialogue, having helped her mother in the kennels on weekends for as long as she could remember. Besides, her mother's rates weren't cheap, but she wanted Jack Beauchamp to know that the guests did get value for money. 'We also provide a television set for those guests who like to watch the soaps,' she explained indulgently. 'As you can see—' she came to a halt as she realized she had lost Jack Beauchamp at the second kennel.

He was down on his haunches in front of the wire mesh door, being rapturously greeted by the Yellow Labrador staying there.

Mattie strolled back to join him, her own expression

softening as she too bent to scratch Sophie behind the ear. 'She's rather lovely, isn't she?' she said quietly, the Labrador having long ago become a favourite of hers.

'Absolutely gorgeous!' Jack Beauchamp turned to grin at her, that flirtatious charm wiped away in his genuine pleasure in the dog's ecstatic greeting. 'And so friendly,' he added warmly.

Mattie's breath caught in her throat at his sudden boyishness. He was just too good-looking for his own good. Or hers!

'Sophie is just pleased to see anyone,' she bit out curtly, instantly realizing how rude she had sounded, but unable to take it back now she had said it. Besides, she did not want to find this man attractive! 'Her elderly owner died three months ago,' she told him grudgingly at his questioning look. 'The family don't want Sophie, and instructed my mother to have her put down. Which is why we still have her.'

There was no way her mother could have a healthy animal put to sleep—which was how they had ended up with four dogs of their own, already! No way could she send Sophie to a dogs' home either, for the very same reason; Sophie might not find a new owner, and so might possibly meet the same fate.

Ordinarily Sophie would have been out of the kennel following her mother around as she worked, but as her mother had been expecting a visitor—this visitor, as it turned out!—she had put Sophie in one of the kennel rooms just for the afternoon.

'That's terrible.' Jack Beauchamp straightened frowningly, still absently stroking Sophie behind one ear.

'Yes,' Mattie acknowledged heavily, in total agreement with him. Over that, at least! 'If you would like to come this way…' she returned to her brisk, businesslike tone '…I will show you one of the empty rooms so that you can see exactly where—Harry?—will be staying if you decide to book him in for next weekend.' Something Mattie, in spite of her mother's need for business, hoped he wouldn't do. She had already agreed to help her mother over the Easter weekend, which meant she was more than likely to bump into Jack Beauchamp again then!

'It's certainly luxurious,' Jack Beauchamp acknowledged a few minutes later, sitting down in the armchair that stood to one side of the guest room.

'Dogs are such loving, giving creatures, we feel they deserve the best,' Mattie rejoined.

Brown eyes surveyed her unemotionally for several long seconds. 'I agree,' he finally answered. 'Harry is going to love it here.' He stood up. 'I know it must sound slightly strange to you, but Harry has been with me since he was a puppy; he's six now, and he's never been away to kennels before.'

Mattie softened slightly. Having grown up with animals, she had the same weakness for them as her mother did. And there was no doubting that Jack Beauchamp—whatever else he might be!—cared about his dog very much.

'I'm sure he'll be fine here with us,' she assured him as he once again bent down to make a fuss of Sophie. 'Let me take you outside and show you the spaciously individual runs we have for each guest.' She carefully locked the doors behind them as they went back outside. 'Although each dog is taken for a long walk every day too,' she hastened to add.

Jack Beauchamp gave that disarming grin once again. 'This is more comfortable than some human hotels!'

'Yes,' Mattie acknowledged ruefully. It had taken a lot of capital to build this luxurious boarding-kennels in the first place, took even more for its upkeep, but it certainly was a first-class hotel for canines.

He quirked dark brows. 'Do you and your mother run it on your own, or do you have help?' he asked conversationally as they strolled back to the front office.

'We have help,' Mattie answered evasively. 'But I'm sure you'll agree, it's a beautiful setting?' she deliberately changed the subject. After all, it was really none of this man's business whether or not she helped her mother on a full-time basis.

It *was* a beautiful setting too. Only a few miles outside London, they were nevertheless surrounded by countryside, their own large garden a riot of spring flowers.

'Beautiful,' he murmured in agreement.

Mattie turned to look at him, her breath catching in her throat as she saw Jack Beauchamp wasn't looking at the garden at all, but at her!

Well, really!

She stiffened resentfully. 'I'll pass you over to my mother now, so that the two of you can sort out the details for your pet's stay,' she told him briskly as they re-entered the office. Her mother looked up with a smile, Mattie's barely perceptible nod of confirmation erasing some of the anxiety from her eyes.

'I hope you found everything to your liking, Mr Beauchamp?' Her mother smiled at him warmly.

'Everything,' he confirmed softly.

Once again Mattie looked up to find him looking at her rather than her mother. He was doing it again!

'And please call me Jack,' he invited her mother.

'Diana,' her mother returned happily, obviously feeling none of the awkwardness around this attractive man that Mattie obviously did.

Of course her mother was about ten years older than Jack Beauchamp, whereas Mattie was around ten years younger. But even so, her mother was still an attractive woman, had also been a widow for a very long time. Admittedly her mother had always claimed to have loved Mattie's father too much to ever become involved again, but surely a woman would have to be almost dead herself not to be aware of Jack Beauchamp's good looks?

'Exactly how did you come to hear of The Woofdorf, Jack?' her mother continued conversationally, the complete professional when it came to her beloved boarding-kennels. 'It's always nice to know these things. Was it a personal recommendation, or did you perhaps see one of our ads—?'

'Strangely enough I found some of your cards lying around in the office. I have no idea who could have put them there.'

Mattie suddenly became very interested in the dozens of photographs that adorned one of the walls of the office, hoping that neither her mother, nor Jack Beauchamp, had noticed how anxious she'd suddenly become.

'Obviously a lucky find,' he acknowledged warmly.

'Obviously,' her mother agreed; no doubt thinking, for us as well as Jack Beauchamp.

He nodded. 'I was explaining to your daughter earlier that Harry has never been away to kennels before—even one as luxurious as this,' he allowed. 'It's just that I really have to be in Paris next weekend, and as the whole family is going, there just isn't anyone left here who I can leave him with, as I usually do when I have to go away. I have to admit—' he grimaced '—that I've left it this late in booking because I've been putting off the evil day for as long as possible.'

Family? What family? Surely this man wasn't *married*, too?

'Every owner feels as you do the first time, Jack,' her mother told him kindly. 'But I do assure you, we will take very good care of Harry. If—'

'I hope you'll both excuse me,' Mattie cut in abruptly, suddenly *really* anxious to get away from the company of this particular man. 'I—I really must go and—and—er—I have some things to do,' she finished lamely.

But Jack Beauchamp had paused in the doorway on his way in, and was still effectively blocking Mattie's exit as she turned to leave. 'I must thank you for showing me round,' he told her quietly. 'It was very nice meeting you, Miss Crawford.'

She looked up at him unblinkingly. 'And you, Mr Beauchamp,' she returned politely—if insincerely. Obviously she didn't merit the privilege of being asked to call him by his first name! Which was okay with her—she would probably have choked on it, anyway.

He smiled, laughter still lurking in the depths of those dark brown eyes—as if he were well aware of her chagrin at the omission. 'I do hope we'll meet again,' he finally said softly.

Contrarily, Mattie hoped for no such thing. Although, in the circumstances, she knew it was a pretty useless hope.

'Probably next weekend—if you do decide to bring

Harry to us,' she dismissed briskly. 'Now, if you will
excuse me…?' She looked at him pointedly as he still
blocked her exit.

'Certainly.' He stepped neatly aside.

Mattie couldn't get out of the room fast enough. Her
chest felt as if it were going to explode from lack of air.

So that was Jack Beauchamp.

Well, he was good-looking enough, she would give
him that. Charming too, if you ignored all that staring
he did. Her mother appeared to like him too. But then,
her mother liked and trusted nearly everyone, even the
young kennel-maid who had stolen money from her the
previous year, so that was no recommendation, either.

But how could Mattie possibly have even guessed that
her leaving those cards for The Woofdorf all over the
offices of JB Industries would result in the man himself
turning up here to board his dog over the Easter weekend? She couldn't, came the obvious answer.

But she was certainly going to have some explaining
to do to her mother once Jack Beauchamp had left!

Because the man she had described to her mother earlier as a womaniser and a greedy pig—and even he had
suggested, albeit mockingly—that such a man should be
taken out into the streets and publicly whipped, was
none other than Jack Beauchamp himself!

CHAPTER TWO

'WHAT an absolutely charming man,' Mattie's mother turned from waving to Jack as he drove away in the red sports car a little time later.

Mattie had very good reason for thinking otherwise. And, in all fairness to her mother, Mattie thought, perhaps she ought to tell her what those reasons were.

'So natural and friendly, despite his obvious wealth. No side to him, as your grandfather would have said,' Diana added affectionately. 'Anyway, he's booked Harry in for four days over the Easter holiday, so we're almost fully booked up now for that period. I have to admit— Mattie, what is it?' She suddenly seemed to become aware of her daughter's less-than-enthusiastic expression.

Confirming that Mattie looked as sick as she felt! Because only an hour ago she had been describing that charming man in a totally different way to her mother. Not that Mattie went back on one single thing she had previously said about Jack Beauchamp, she just knew she wouldn't be able to leave her mother in ignorance as to his identity.

She drew in a deep breath. 'I had no idea you pronounced the name Beauchamp as Beecham,' she began slowly. 'If I had I—well, I—' She would have what? No matter how you pronounced the man's name, he was still everything she had said he was; not only did he

18

have four girlfriends that she already knew about, but it turned out he had a family of his own too!

'Mattie…?' Her mother frowned at her suspiciously. 'Mattie, what have you done?' she prompted warily.

'Done?' Mattie repeated, her voice slightly higher than usual, then clearing her throat to bring it down in tone. 'What makes you think I've done something?' she said over-brightly, deciding that coming clean to her mother wasn't going to be easy to do, after all.

'Because I know you too well, Mattie,' her mother admitted worriedly. 'I also know that you've been getting into one scrape or another all your life… What does it matter how you pronounce Jack Beauchamp's name?' she asked slowly.

It mattered a lot when you glanced in your mother's appointment book for today and saw no connection between the name Jack Beecham—her mother had obviously spelt the name as it had been spoken to her over the telephone—and Jonathan Beauchamp, of JB Industries!

'It doesn't,' she sighed. 'Not really. But— Oh, Mum, you're right; I've done something awful!' She gave a pained grimace.

And when Jack Beauchamp found out exactly what it was she had done he was unlikely to bring his dog anywhere near her mother's boarding-kennels!

'Do you want to talk about it?' her mother pressed gently; accustomed over the years to her daughter's acts of impetuosity—followed by Mattie's inevitable feelings of regret.

Talking about it was the very last thing Mattie wanted to do! But she really didn't have a choice in this case. 'I suppose I'll have to.' She sighed heavily.

'Does it merit coffee or hot chocolate?' her mother probed; in the past, coffee had always been chosen for a minor indiscretion, hot chocolate for a really major one!

Mattie looked forlorn. 'In all honesty, I think this one may call for a glass of whisky!'

Her mother's blonde brows rose almost to her hairline; none of Mattie's confessions had ever merited whisky before! But over the years there had certainly been a lot of them; more often than not the impulsive Mattie acted first and thought later. This definitely sounded like one of those occasions.

'Back to the house, I think,' her mother decided ruefully.

Mattie followed reluctantly, knowing the next few minutes were going to be far from pleasant. Not least because she now suspected her mother might have been right in her initial summing up of the situation. Mattie probably had overreacted to Jonathan Beauchamp—because of the two-timing Richard!

Not that she had changed her mind about Jonathan Beauchamp's behaviour—not in the least!—but maybe she wouldn't have done quite what she *had* done if it weren't for her own humiliating experience where Richard had been concerned.

Her mother made them both tea rather than the suggested whisky, the two of them sitting down at the table in their cluttered but comfortable kitchen, four dogs milling affectionately around their feet.

'Well, Matilda-May?' her mother prompted after several minutes of Mattie sitting staring broodingly into her teacup.

Mattie winced at the use of her full name. 'I wish you

wouldn't call me that,' she protested. 'In fact, I think it was very unkind of you to name me that at all. Just because your mother was named Matilda, and Dad's was called May, was really no reason—'

'Mattie, you can delay this as long as you like,' her mother cut in crisply, 'but in the end you're still going to have to tell me what it is you've done,' she reasoned.

Mattie swallowed hard, sighing deeply before speaking. 'You remember the womaniser?'

'The woma—? Oh, you mean the man you were telling me about earlier, the one who has four girlfriends?' her mother recalled.

'That's the one,' Mattie confirmed awkwardly. 'Well, Jack Beauchamp is Jonathan Beauchamp!' she burst out. 'Him. It. He's the womaniser!' she revealed reluctantly. 'What I mean is—'

'I think I get your drift, Mattie,' her mother acknowledged dryly. 'He's the man you were so angry about earlier today? The man whose secretary placed his order with you yesterday to send out four bouquets to his numerous girlfriends?'

Mattie took a quick swallow of her tea, burning her mouth in the process. But, in the circumstances, she decided, she probably deserved the discomfort!

How could she have been so stupid? So unprofessional? At the time she had thought she was being so clever; having now met Jack Beauchamp she had no idea how he was going to react to what she had done. But she could probably take a pretty good guess...!

So much for her own job of running a successful florists, for some lucrative contracts she also had to service the plants and greenery at half a dozen office complexes—JB Industries being one of them. And Jack Beauchamp *was* JB Industries!

If he decided to turn nasty over what she had done, she might just find herself losing all of those contracts, and the florist's shop too! As for her mother being allowed to look after the man's dog—!

'Yes,' Mattie confirmed flatly.

'But you dealt with his order, didn't you?' Her mother looked puzzled.

'Oh, I dealt with it, all right,' Mattie agreed, giving another wince at what else she had done. 'You see, I had delivered four bouquets for him to those four women at Christmas—'

'I suppose that shows he's been involved with the same four women for the last four months at least,' her mother reasoned.

'The thing is,' Mattie began reluctantly, 'his secretary gave me the order, and he—he had already written out four cards to go with each bouquet. And I—Mum—I changed the cards around!' she admitted guiltily, utterly dismayed herself now to realize exactly what she had done.

She was twenty-three years old; it was high time she stopped *doing* things like this!

'And he wasn't even original,' she continued in her own defence as her mother looked stunned by the admission. 'He had written "Sandy, much love, J", "Tina, much love, J", "Sally, much love, J", and "Cally, much love, J", and so I—well, I thought perhaps they ought to be made aware of each other's existence. So I put Tina's card in with Cally's bouquet, Sandy's card in with Tina's, Sally's card in with Sandy's, and Cally's in with Sally's. I know it was a stupid thing to do, but I—

Mum, you aren't crying, are you?' She looked worriedly across the table at her mother as she suddenly buried her face in her hands, her shoulders shaking emotionally. 'I'll go to him, I'll explain what I did, tell him—' Mattie broke off as her mother dropped her hands to look across at her, her own eyes widening incredulously as she saw her mother was laughing, not crying!

'Oh, Mattie, *Mattie*.' Her mother shook her head, still choked with laughter. 'You most certainly will have to go and explain things to him. Quite how you're going to do that, I have no idea.' She sobered slightly. 'I thought the Richard incident was disastrous, expected his fiancée to turn up on our doorstep demanding an explanation right up to the morning of the wedding!' She shook her head wearily. 'But this…!'

'Be fair, Mum,' Mattie protested. 'The Richard thing wasn't exactly my fault. There was no way I could have guessed he was already engaged.'

'No,' her mother acceded with affection. 'But, you have to admit, this latest escapade is certainly the biggest Mattie mess-up so far.' She gave another shake of her head as she obviously tried to contain the laughter.

So far? After this Mattie never intended interfering again! Ever!

'It isn't funny, Mum,' she responded reprovingly at her mother as Diana lost the battle with her laughter and began to chuckle once again.

'No, it isn't,' her mother agreed, tears of laughter falling softly down her cheeks now.

'Then I wish you would stop laughing!' Mattie sighed, then even her own mouth began to twitch with the same laughter. 'He's going to kill me,' she realized. 'String me up by my thumbs. Hang me from the nearest tree—'

'Darling, if he does the first one he really won't need to bother with the second and third,' her mother reasoned, wiping the dampness from her cheeks with a tissue before offering the box to Mattie.

'He looks the type who would do them just for the fun of it!' Mattie muttered, blowing her nose noisily with one of the tissues, not sure now whether she wanted to laugh or cry herself; Jack Beauchamp, if he chose, had the power to ruin her!

Her mother gave a rueful shake of her head. 'I suppose you did definitely deliver those bouquets yesterday?'

But they both knew her question was rhetorical. Mattie made a point of always delivering bouquets and floral arrangements at the time requested. It was one of the reasons that she had so many regular customers. Although she doubted she would be able to continue to list Jack Beauchamp amongst their number after this weekend's deliberate mix-up!

'If it's any consolation, Mattie, Jack Beauchamp wasn't sporting any visible wounds this afternoon that could have been given to him by an outraged girlfriend!' Her mother grinned.

'It isn't,' Mattie returned heavily; she might feel a little less devastated if she knew something positive had resulted from her—she admitted it now!—latest reckless action. A black eye, at least from one of the women might have made her feel her actions had been justified! 'I absolutely hate the thought of having to go to the man and telling him what I've done,' she admitted.

Her mother nodded. 'Having met Jack Beauchamp, I can understand that. But I also have a feeling that if you don't go and see him then he'll be coming in to the florist's to see you tomorrow, anyway!'

Mattie had the same feeling. And it was probably better to be at least half in charge of the situation rather than completely on the defensive. Besides, this didn't just affect her; possibly she had also jeopardized her mother's booking to board Jack Beauchamp's dog over the Easter weekend.

The weekend. When he was going away to Paris with his family.

His family...

Maybe she wouldn't have to go quite so apologetically on bended knee, after all; if Jack Beauchamp already had a wife and family, then he shouldn't be sending flowers to other women in the first place!

She began to hope that, perhaps, she might be able to salvage her own professional reputation from this mess, after all. Jack Beauchamp could hardly make too much of a fuss over those wrongly addressed cards on the flowers without causing some domestic discomfort to himself.

Better to think positively, she told herself firmly. After all, what could the man really do to her...?

She felt rather less sure of herself the following day when she faced Jack Beauchamp across the width of the imposing desk in his equally impressive office!

She had intended going to his home the previous evening, but the address and telephone number he had given her mother were those of his offices in the City, leaving Mattie with no choice but to wait until Monday to speak to him.

She had worried all evening, and hardly slept through

the night, as she imagined at least *one* of his girlfriends having contacted him concerning the wrongly named card attached to her bouquet.

Her mother had looked at her across the breakfast table this morning, had taken in at a glance the heaviness of Mattie's eyes, and the strained look on her face, handed her a cup of coffee, and, without speaking a word, gone outside to feed her canine guests.

Which was just as well, because Mattie hadn't felt like talking. Not that she felt like talking now, either, but she knew she didn't have any choice in the matter this time!

It didn't help that Jack Beauchamp looked much less approachable today in a dark business suit, cream shirt, and neatly knotted tie, than he had when he'd visited the boarding-kennels yesterday.

But he looked calm enough—he didn't have the look of a man whose personal life was imploding!

Oh, well, she chivvied herself along even as she drew in a deep breath, she might as well get this over with; delaying any further wasn't going to make it any easier.

'Mr Beauchamp—'

'Jack,' he invited lightly, sitting back in his high-backed leather chair to look across at her assessingly.

Now why couldn't he have been more friendly yesterday, Mattie thought to herself. Not that it would have made her confession today any easier, but it would certainly have been more pleasant—

'My secretary explained that when you phoned first thing this morning you said it was urgent you see me today.' Jack Beauchamp sat forward to rest his arms on the desk.

Of course Mattie had said it was urgent that she needed to see him—once she had told Claire Thomas who she was, because that was the only way the other woman would agree to fit her into Mr Beauchamp's busy schedule for a few minutes before lunch. Although, Mattie had been warned, Jack Beauchamp did have an appointment at one o'clock.

As it was ten minutes to that hour now, she had better get this over with!

'Is there a problem with Harry's booking for the weekend?' Jack Beauchamp frowned.

'Not that I know of,' Mattie dismissed hastily. 'I— I'm not here in my capacity as my mother's assistant.'

Dark brows rose over chocolate-brown eyes as Jack Beauchamp's expression became speculative now. 'No?' he drawled, some of yesterday's warmth returning to those come-to-bed eyes. 'Then why is it so urgent that you see me?'

Certainly not for the reason he seemed to be imagining, Mattie thought impatiently. Really, the man was back in seduction mode again!

She had deliberately dressed in a businesslike way herself today, in a navy blue suit and pale blue blouse, in the hope that it might give her the necessary boost of confidence she needed to tell him about the mix-up with the cards. As she felt the dampness of her palms, the inner panic that made her want to turn tail and run, she knew that ploy had failed utterly!

She grimaced. 'I don't actually work at the boarding-kennels, Mr—er, Jack,' she corrected herself. Try and keep this pleasant, she instructed herself firmly.

Who knew? There was always the possibility that he would see the funny side of this.

Oh, yes? she instantly taunted herself. In the same circumstances, would she?

No, of course not—but then she would never have got herself into such a romantic tangle in the first place. But hadn't she done exactly that—albeit unwillingly—with Richard…?

'You don't?' Jonathan Beauchamp mused softly now. 'Then exactly what is it that you do, Mattie?'

He had known her first name all the time! Well…probably not all the time, she conceded, but no doubt her mother had casually dropped it into their conversation somewhere yesterday. And yet he had insisted on continuing to use the formality of her surname… Not a good sign!

'I actually work for you—well, not exactly,' she amended, 'but you are one of my clients, and—'

'Mattie, could you stop and go back a few steps?' he interrupted her, laughter now lurking in those warm brown eyes and around those finely chiselled lips. 'Before I go off on completely the wrong tangent, perhaps you had better tell me exactly what your profession is?'

What did he mean, a wrong tangent? Exactly what did he imagine—?

'I'm a florist, Mr Beauchamp!' she told him coldly as a certain profession sprang to mind. 'I am the proprietor of Green and Beautiful,' she added for good measure, glaring at him as her thoughts lingered briefly on that other profession.

How dared he—? How could he—? Did she *look* like—?

Mattie's mind went blank, her mouth dry, as she saw the dawning realization on his face—a face that was rapidly darkening with what looked suspiciously like—

'Ah,' he said slowly—as if he had suddenly been given the answer to a riddle that had been bothering him.

'In that case, could this urgent need to see me today possibly have anything to do with the mix-up concerning the cards I requested be included with the delivery of certain bouquets over the weekend…?'

At least one of those four women had been in contact with him, after all!

Mattie was sure she must have a sick expression back on her face. If only—

'I was actually going to contact you myself later to-day,' Jack Beauchamp continued, no warmth in that chocolate-brown gaze now—in fact, his whole expression had suddenly become enigmatically unreadable.

'I had a feeling you might,' Mattie acknowledged quickly.

'And you thought you would circumvent that visit by coming here to see me instead?' he prompted in that silkily soft voice.

'Yes,' she confirmed abruptly. 'You see, I—I was checking through some papers yesterday evening, and realized I had made a terrible mistake—'

'Did you indeed…?' he interjected, standing up to move around the desk with surprising speed for such a large man. 'Exactly *when* yesterday did you say you had realized your error?'

Even wearing two-inch heels Mattie had to tilt her head back to look up into his face. Not that she was sure she wanted to! He was altogether too close, and she really had no idea what his mood was. Although she was sure it couldn't be pleasant, not after the havoc she had probably wreaked in his personal life!

'I told you, it was yesterday evening. I really am sorry—'

'Mattie, interesting as this conversation undoubtedly

is, could we possibly continue it over dinner this evening?' he cut in after a brief glance at his wrist-watch. 'You see, I have a luncheon appointment in two minutes, and—'

'No, we could not continue this conversation—or indeed, anything!—over dinner!' Mattie burst out disbelievingly. In fact, she couldn't believe he had actually asked her that!

He raised dark brows. 'No?'

'No!' she snapped incredulously.

'Why not?' he pressed.

Her eyes blazed deeply blue. 'For one thing—you're a married man!' she reminded him forcefully. 'For another—you already have at least four girlfriends that I know of!'

There, she had said it. So much for coming here and claiming the mix-up with the cards had been a simple mistake—which was the excuse she had come up with during her wakeful hours early this morning. But what else was she supposed to do when the man was now actually daring to try and add her to his list of women?

She glanced up at him, quickly looking away again as she realized he was standing much too close to her. With the desk behind her, and Jack Beauchamp standing in front of her, she had no means of escape if he should—

'Jack…? Am I too early for our luncheon appointment?'

Mattie gave a nervous start at the sound of an intrusive female voice, at the same time acknowledging that she and Jack Beauchamp must have been so intent on each other that neither of them had heard the other woman open the door and enter the room.

Jack Beauchamp's eyes narrowed on Mattie briefly before he stepped away from her, a smile curving his lips now as he turned to greet the other woman. 'Not at all,' he assured her smoothly. 'Mattie and I were just finalizing our arrangements for this evening,' he added with a pointed glare in Mattie's direction.

A glare Mattie was totally immune to, her whole attention focused on the tall woman who had just entered the office.

She was beautiful, her luxuriously thick hair falling in ebony waves to just below her slender shoulders, blue eyes sparkling with health and vitality, make-up understated on the ravishing beauty of her face. The fitted blue dress she wore—expensive by its cut—was the exact same colour as her eyes, her legs looked long and silky, her feet small and delicate in strappy black sandals.

'Mattie.' Jack Beauchamp took a firm hold of her arm as he pulled her forward to stand at his side. 'Let me introduce you to my sister, Alexandra.'

His sister? Did he really expect her to believe that?

The other woman gave a questioning look in Jack Beauchamp's direction before turning to Mattie. 'Lovely to meet you, Mattie.' She smiled warmly, her voice huskily attractive. 'I do apologize if I'm interrupting,' she added. 'Claire wasn't in her office outside, so I let myself in.'

'Not at all,' Mattie assured her nervously, wishing Jack Beauchamp would let go of her arm. It wasn't that he was particularly hurting her, she just wasn't comfortable with the tingling sensation that was moving from her wrist to her shoulder! 'I was just leaving, anyway,' she excused, deliberately stepping away from Jack

Beauchamp so that he had no choice but to release her arm.

Except that he didn't, his dark gaze challenging on hers as he maintained his grip. 'We haven't settled the details for this evening,' he insisted. 'You said dinner is out, so how about I pick you up about nine o'clock and we go and have a quiet drink together somewhere?'

How about they just forgot about the whole thing?

Except, Mattie realised Jack Beauchamp didn't intend letting her off that easily.

'Okay,' she finally agreed reluctantly. 'If that's what you want to do.'

'It's what I want to do, Mattie,' he echoed decisively.

'Fine,' she snapped, looking down to where his hand still clasped her arm, taking a relieved step back as he finally released her. 'Until nine o'clock this evening, then,' she muttered.

He gave a slight inclination of his head. 'I'm looking forward to it.'

Well, Mattie certainly wasn't!

What was he going to say to her? More to the point, what was he going to do about her act of sabotage on his personal life?

CHAPTER THREE

'YOU changed those name cards over on purpose, didn't you?'

Mattie, in the process of taking a sip of her glass of white wine, swallowed too hastily, the liquid going down the wrong way and choking her.

She coughed and spluttered, the wine instantly going up her nose as well as down her windpipe, her eyes and nose watering as she tried to control herself.

'Here.' Jack reached over and gave her a helpful slap on the back as he sat beside her in the corner booth of the country pub he had driven them to.

Almost knocking Mattie off the seat in the process!

Had there been any need to slap her on the back quite that hard? Mattie didn't think so. Besides, it hadn't helped—she was still coughing and spluttering, several people in the bar turning to give her sympathetic looks.

Which was more than Jack Beauchamp was doing—amusement seemed to be the main emotion in those laughing brown eyes and the curve of his mouth!

'Blow your nose,' Jack instructed dryly, handing her a snowy white handkerchief.

Mattie did so. Noisily. And it did help. Only her eyes were watering now.

'Feeling better?' Jack enquired as she mopped up the moisture from her face and eyes, at the same time sure that her mascara must have run down her cheeks.

Yes, it had, she realized with an inward groan as she

looked down at what had once been a pristine white handkerchief, but which was now streaked with brown stains. Oh, well, the way she looked was the least of her problems!

And how could she possibly be feeling better after what he had just said to her? He knew she had swapped those cards over on purpose!

'Thank you,' she said tautly, crushing the handkerchief in the palm of her hand; she doubted he would want it back now that she had blown her nose on it!

Jack Beauchamp had arrived at the bungalow promptly at nine o'clock this evening. Which was just as well—because Mattie had been standing at the end of the driveway waiting for him. She didn't want him any nearer in case he alerted her mother as to whom she was spending the evening with.

She had assured her mother, when she'd arrived home from work a few hours earlier, that the situation with Jack Beauchamp had been settled, that he accepted her explanation of a mistake being made, that he wouldn't be cancelling his booking for Harry this weekend. All she had to do then was convince Jack Beauchamp of that!

His opening comment had seemed to put an end to that particular hope.

She cleared her throat noisily before speaking. 'I did try to explain to you earlier—' before his luncheon date arrived! '—that I had realized my mistake over the weekend—'

'You did,' he conceded dryly. 'But your subsequent remark about a wife and four girlfriends seemed to imply something else.' He quirked dark brows over mocking eyes.

Mattie winced as she clearly remembered making that particular comment in his office earlier.

'Don't you think?' he prompted mildly before sipping the half-pint of beer he had ordered for his own drink.

Perhaps if she had thought more before delivering those flowers on Saturday— But that was her problem: she didn't think, just acted!

She wished she didn't have to think now, either! Because the more she thought about what she had done, the more she realized just how completely unprofessionally she had behaved. It was none of her business if one of her clients had a dozen girlfriends who had no idea of each other's existence; she was just paid to deliver flowers, not make moral judgements. Or act on the latter!

'You see, Mattie.' Jack spoke pleasantly as he turned more fully towards her.

To the onlooker it would have seemed as if he just wanted to get closer to her. But Mattie easily recognized he had trapped her more securely in her corner seat. Not that she was thinking of running anyway. She wasn't stupid enough to think she would get very far; Jack Beauchamp might spend his weekdays sitting behind a desk, but he had the physique of a sportsman.

'I've also been thinking about the conversation I overheard you having with your mother when I arrived at the boarding-kennels yesterday afternoon,' he continued determinedly. 'I believe you were discussing a womaniser and a greedy pig…? The greedy pig in question apparently having four girlfriends?'

Mattie's heart sank even more. It must be in her shoes by now!

She moistened dry lips—surprisingly so, considering all the wine she had spluttered over herself seconds ago!

It didn't help that the damned man looked so attractive. She had deliberately dressed casually herself, in faded denims and a white tee shirt with 'Sexy' printed on the front, in the hope of playing down the importance of this meeting. But Jack Beauchamp was dressed just as casually, also in faded denims, his own rugby-style top just making him look more athletic. In fact, he should be the one wearing a tee shirt that said 'Sexy'— as a warning to women to beware!

And the last thing she should be thinking about right now was how attractive the man was. The problem was, she just didn't know what to say in answer to this frontal attack!

'Oh, come on, Mattie,' he chided. 'You didn't seem to have too much trouble articulating your feelings yesterday.'

'Or tonight, either!' she snapped, stung into replying now. 'Okay, so that was you I was discussing with my mother yesterday, but that doesn't mean—doesn't mean—'

'Yes?' he pushed.

She glared at him. 'I made a mistake, okay?' she bit out at him resentfully. 'Everyone makes mistakes occasionally.' Even you, her tone implied.

'So they do,' he acknowledged in that too-mild voice. 'But which mistake of yours are we referring to?'

This was actually a really nice pub, out in the country, with an olde-worlde atmosphere that seemed natural rather than contrived. There was a very attractive man sitting at her side and in other circumstances Mattie would have enjoyed herself. In other circumstances…

'Look, I was the one who came to see you this morning, with the intention of apologizing for my mistake, and—and—'

'Yes?' Jack prompted as she broke off to look at him quizzically.

'What do you mean, which mistake of mine?' Mattie frowned.

'Ah.' He gave a humourless smile. 'So you've finally realized that you may have made more than one.'

The only one that she could see was in daring to challenge this man—which, she freely admitted, was definitely a mistake! But Jack seemed to be implying she had got something else wrong...?

'You mentioned your family yesterday,' she began again slowly. 'I assumed you meant a wife and children...?'

'No wife. No children,' he told her evenly. 'Parents. And several siblings. One of which you met earlier today.'

Mattie looked sceptical. 'And they are the family you're going away with to Paris this weekend?' He couldn't really expect her to believe that explanation! Paris was a place for lovers, not for a man in his early thirties to visit with his parents and siblings!

He nodded, totally unconcerned by her obvious scepticism. 'My youngest sister—Alexandra; you met her earlier,' he reminded her.

'Yes...' Mattie agreed, still not convinced about that particular relationship.

He shrugged. 'She recently became engaged, and decided that she would like to have her celebration dinner at the restaurant on the Eiffel Tower.'

Mattie didn't know whether to laugh at the absurdity of this explanation, or to feel envious that someone could actually decide such a thing—and then it happened! Whichever way, it sounded highly unlikely to her.

'So you don't have a wife,' Mattie accepted; maybe she could concede she might have been wrong about that.

'Or four girlfriends,' Jack Beauchamp told her firmly.

'Well…probably not any more!' Mattie couldn't hold back her grin.

He still wasn't sporting any visible signs of having recently encountered a woman—or indeed four women!—scorned, but for a man with a number of girlfriends he didn't seem to have had any problem finding himself free to see her this evening!

'Do you know what I think, Mattie?' he spoke consideringly. 'I think your father should have smacked your bottom more when you were a little girl!' he continued, before she had time to think of a wisecrack answer concerning her lack of interest in what he thought about anything.

Her smile faded. 'That might have been a little difficult—you see, he died when I was three,' she explained evenly.

She had only vague memories of her father, a tall man who had used to throw her over his shoulder and carry her up to bed, a man who had always been laughing. She remembered her mother had always seemed to be laughing in those days too…

'I'm sorry.' Jack Beauchamp's quiet apology brought her back to an awareness of where she was—and exactly who she was with. 'That must have been difficult for you.'

'More so for my mother, I would think,' Mattie replied, giving a dismissive shrug to hide the pain talk of her father's premature death could still cause her.

'Yes…'

Mattie waited for Jack to carry on with his earlier rebuke, and when he didn't she turned to look at him. He was obviously deep in thought, although his enigmatic expression made it impossible to even guess what those thoughts were about. As long as he wasn't feeling sorry for her because of her father—

'You see, Mattie,' he suddenly rasped, 'your recent—behaviour, has put me in something of an awkward position.'

'Oh, yes?' she prompted warily—she didn't need to ask which part of her behaviour he was talking about; Jack Beauchamp no more believed her story about it being a genuine mistake, that she had mixed up the cards that had accompanied his bouquets, than she did his claim about those four women not being his girlfriends!

'Oh, yes,' he confirmed dryly, turning to look at her once again. 'Of course, there is a way round it…'

Why did Mattie suddenly have the feeling that she wasn't going to like his way round his particular problem?

Although there was no way she could possibly have been prepared for his next question!

'Do you have a valid passport?'

'Do I have a what?' she gasped incredulously.

'A valid passport,' Jack repeated calmly.

'Well, yes, I— What do you want to know that for?' she demanded suspiciously; she had acquired a passport for the first time the previous year, when she and her mother had managed to get away, for the first time in years, to Greece for a week's holiday. But what business was it of Jack Beauchamp's whether or not she had a valid passport?

'I've explained to you that I'm going to Paris this weekend,' he reminded her.

'For your sister's engagement dinner...' she recalled slowly.

'Well, I wasn't going alone,' he told her with an air of regret.

'You mentioned your parents and siblings are all going to be there too—'

'No, Mattie,' Jack Beauchamp drawled mockingly. 'I meant *I* wasn't going alone. And if you have a valid passport, I'm still not.'

'I don't— Ah.' She winced as his meaning suddenly became clear. Obviously one of those four women he had sent flowers to over the weekend had been going to Paris with him.

Had been... Because after what Mattie had done with the cards she doubted any of those women were still speaking to him, let alone going to Paris for any weekend with him! Which meant it had to have been the unmarried one. Now which one had she been, Sally or Sandy or—

Did it really matter? Mattie instantly chided herself; Jack Beauchamp seemed to be telling her, with his question concerning her own passport, that, now she had put paid to his original companion for his weekend, she would have to accompany him instead!

'I don't think so, Mr Beauchamp,' she told him loftily. Exactly what did he think she was? She sold and delivered flowers; she did not hire herself out for weekends in Paris!

'You don't?'

'No, I don't!' Her voice rose indignantly, eyes flashing deeply blue.

'Paris in the spring,' he teased. 'What could be more romantic?'

Mattie frowned at him reprovingly for his levity. 'Okay, so I accept I've rather messed things up for you this weekend, but I'm sure that with your looks and apparent charm—' after all, he had to have something to have acquired four girlfriends in the first place! '—you can easily find another woman to take to Paris!' Most women she knew would jump at the chance—and not just because there was a trip to the French capital on offer.

Much as she hated to admit it, Jack Beauchamp was extremely attractive to look at, and he did possess a lazy charm that made her feel totally feminine. Not that *she* was in the least charmed, she told herself firmly; the man was just an accomplished flirt.

'A bit short notice, don't you think?' he parried.

Mattie shrugged. 'I'm sure you'll manage to think of something.'

'So you think I have looks and charm?' he enquired.

'As far as some women are concerned!' she retorted. Heaven forbid he should gain the impression she found him the least bit attractive.

Even if she did...

It would be very hard for any woman not to acknowledge that he was extremely good-looking. It was just his having four girlfriends at the same time that was so unattractive. Just! As far as Mattie was concerned, especially after the Richard incident, it was totally unacceptable.

'But you've very effectively put an end to all that, Mattie,' he reminded her.

So her plan had worked, after all!

She shook her head. 'That doesn't mean I have to take their place as an act of appeasement!'

He chuckled softly. 'I wasn't suggesting you should sleep with me while we're in Paris, Mattie—'

'I told you, I am not going to Paris with you!' she told him with firm finality.

While, at the same time, her imagination ran amuck with visions of Jack Beauchamp and herself, locked languidly together, their naked bodies passionately entwined as they kissed and caressed each other...

'I doubt we would do much sleeping if we were to share a bedroom anywhere, Mattie,' Jack's murmured comment interrupted her intimate imaginings.

Mattie looked at him sharply, her blush deepening to embarrassment as she wondered if some of her inner thoughts had been visible on her face. She sincerely hoped not!

She swallowed hard, avoiding that warm dark gaze now. 'I don't see what the problem is with your going to Paris on your own,' she dismissed scathingly. 'Surely you can do without some adoring female in tow for one weekend?' she derided. 'Besides, you said it's all going to be your family there, anyway—'

'And Thom's. My sister's fiancé,' he explained at Mattie's puzzled glance. 'Thom's parents will be there. Also his sister.'

Mattie hesitated. The way he made that last statement, the deliberateness of his tone, seemed to imply—

'Not another one!' she sighed disgustedly; really, did

the man have no scruples whatsoever? On the evidence she had seen so far, obviously not!

'Not as far as I'm concerned, no,' he told her dryly.

Mattie's gaze narrowed at his claim. 'But Thom's sister has other ideas…?'

Jack nodded. 'It's completely unreciprocated, Mattie, I can assure you,' he told her wryly. 'But as Sharon is Thom's sister, it's rather an awkward situation. Short of actually telling her I'm just not interested, which would make things very difficult for everyone—I thought that if I turned up in Paris with a female in tow—'

'Thanks very much!' Mattie protested.

'You weren't my original choice,' he reminded her.

No, either Sally, Cally, Sandy, or Tina had been that. But as Mattie, with one of her impulsive actions, had put paid to any of them going to Paris with him—!

'What's wrong with this Sharon?' she prompted interestedly.

'I'm too much of a gentleman to say,' Jack returned smoothly.

Just as well she wasn't taking another sip of her wine when he said that! Gentleman, indeed!

Mattie shook her head. 'I have a business to run, I can't just disappear off to Paris for three days—'

'Four,' Jack corrected evenly. 'And Friday and Monday are bank holidays,' he reasoned. 'So it will only be for the Saturday. I'm sure you must take time off; who looks after the shop then?'

She didn't very often take holidays, but when she did she always called on her best friend Sam from their university days. Sam was married with a young baby now, but she loved to keep her hand in and work in the shop if she had the chance. Except Mattie really didn't want to take this particular holiday!

'It doesn't matter how many days it is—I'm not going!' Mattie repeated firmly.

'No?' He raised dark brows.

Mattie took a desperate swallow of her wine, managing to avoid choking herself this time, although the warmth of the alcohol did nothing to fill the cold hollow she could feel in the pit of her stomach.

Her deliberate act—an act Jack Beauchamp knew to be deliberate!—in changing those cards on the flowers he'd sent to the four women in his life had been a really stupid, unprofessional thing to do. Something else Jack Beauchamp was well aware of. As he was also aware he could make serious professional trouble for her if he chose to do so...

Blackmail. The man was using blackmail on her. A crime as serious—if not more so—than the one she had committed.

But that was the important thing here—the one she had committed...

Deliberately. Not cold-bloodedly. She had been too indignant, on behalf of those four unsuspecting women—as well as for herself, she admitted now—for it ever to be called that! But she had definitely acted with malice aforethought.

But that surely wasn't punishable, courtesy of a weekend in Paris with this man—

What was she saying? A weekend in Paris with Jack Beauchamp wasn't a punishment. At least, not one that any sane woman would see as punishment... The man was gorgeous, charming, so sexy he made her toes curl to look at him. Punishment! Most women would leap at the chance to go to Paris with him for the weekend.

Even her, if she were honest with herself...

She avoided his teasing gaze, moistening dry lips. 'What would I tell my mother?' Oh, Mattie, she inwardly chided; she knew she wasn't in the least sophisticated, but she could at least try to act as if she were. What would her mother say, indeed!

Jack seemed to give the question serious thought, surprisingly no mockery in his expression as he did so. 'I suppose it's too much to hope that your mother doesn't know I'm the greedy pig you were talking about yesterday?' he finally responded.

Once again Mattie couldn't meet his eyes. 'Er—'

'She knows,' he accepted economically. 'Well, how about telling her the truth about this trip to Paris, then?'

'The truth?' Mattie gasped unbelievingly. 'You want me to tell my mother that you're blackmailing me into accompanying you to Paris because I did a totally unprofessional thing and you could ruin me because of it?'

Jack winced. 'When you put it like that...'

'It was your suggestion I tell her the truth!' Mattie challenged.

He sighed. 'So it was. I just didn't expect the truth to sound—quite like that.' He gave another wince. 'Can't you just tell your mother that you're helping me out as a friend?'

'By going to Paris with you!' Mattie scorned.

'Yes.'

'We aren't friends,' she stated.

'I think we're going to have to be if we intend spending the weekend together with my family,' Jack reasoned lightly.

Mattie stared at him frustratedly. This was farcical. Ludicrous. And yet…

She couldn't pretend that a part of her wasn't curious as to how it would feel to go to Paris with a man like Jack Beauchamp. In fact, she couldn't pretend that a part of her didn't long to go to Paris, with or without Jack Beauchamp!

There had been little time or opportunity for holidays in her one-parent family; during her childhood she and her mother had usually been looking after other people's dogs for them while *they'd* gone on holiday. Besides, there had never been enough money for her mother to splash out on holidays. Except last year, when Mattie had insisted on taking Diana away for a much-needed break, having decided that her mother had done enough for her already. It had been time for Mattie to do something nice for her mum for a change!

She doubted having an unemployed, disgraced daughter could be classed as nice…!

She gave Jack Beauchamp an impatient glance. 'Mr Beauchamp, I think you are utterly despicable—'

'Jack,' he put in easily.

'Whatever your name, you're still despicable!' Mattie's eyes flashed deeply blue.

He grinned. 'Does that mean you're coming to Paris with me?'

Now why on earth had her heart seemed to actually flip over in her chest as he said that? Really, Mattie, she inwardly chastised herself, get a grip!

If she agreed to accompany Jack to Paris it would be because he wanted her there as a deterrent to a woman called Sharon, and for no other reason.

Still…Paris was Paris. And it *was* supposed to be the romantic capital of the world… Besides, hadn't she already half planned her wardrobe inside her head even as she continued to tell Jack Beauchamp she wasn't going with him?

She took a deep breath before nodding. 'It means I'm coming to Paris with you,' she conceded slowly. 'But don't get the impression I'm doing this for any other reason than I was blackmailed into it!' her niggling feelings of guilt at her inner excitement made her add with unnecessary force.

'Of course not,' Jack assured her wryly.

Mattie shot him a sharply searching look. He hadn't exactly sounded convinced…

'Just think, Mattie. Cruising on the Seine,' he crooned. 'Strolling along the Champs-Elysées. The Arc de Triomphe. Coffee at a sidewalk café. Dinner at the Eiffel Tower.'

She couldn't help it, the idea became more and more enticing the longer he spoke. It did sound rather wonderful.

In fact, the only fly in the ointment was that she would have to share it all with Jack Beauchamp!

CHAPTER FOUR

'YOU'RE going *where*? And with *whom*?' Her mother looked across the kitchen at Mattie disbelievingly.

Mattie had waited until breakfast the following morning before attempting to break the news to Diana about the forthcoming weekend. Her mother's response was not encouraging. In fact, Mattie thought Diana looked as if she might drop the mug of coffee she had just stood up to pour for herself!

Mattie gently took the mug out of her mother's hand and put it on the table before disaster struck. 'To Paris,' she mumbled, avoiding her mother's incredulous gaze as she did so. 'With Jack Beauchamp.'

Mattie was still dressed in her pyjamas and dressing-gown, although her mother had already been out this morning and fed her guests their breakfast.

'But we'll have separate bedrooms,' she added quickly, hoping she spoke the truth; as she remembered it, they hadn't quite finished that particular part of their conversation last night…!

'Well, that's a relief,' her mother accepted weakly, sitting down at the kitchen table, giving the impression it was only a short moment before she actually fell down! 'Mattie, is this your idea of sorting out the situation with Jack Beauchamp?'

'Not exactly,' Mattie admitted. 'It's his idea of sorting out the situation with me!'

She took Jack's advice then and told her mother the whole truth. Which took some time.

'As prison sentences go, I didn't think a weekend in Paris was too bad,' she concluded wryly.

Her mother shook her head. 'I don't think—I didn't think—Jack Beauchamp didn't actually— Oh, Mattie, what am I going to do with you?' There were tears in her eyes as she made her age-old cry whenever Mattie got into one of her scrapes. Which was often.

Mattie reached over and clasped her mother's hand. 'It will be all right,' she reassured her warmly. 'After all, you will have the man's dog here to hold for ransom!'

Her mother gave a tearful laugh. 'So I will,' she conceded. 'I just can't believe you're going to Paris with him.' She shook her head dazedly.

'I thought you liked him,' Mattie reminded her.

'I do. I did,' her mother corrected herself. 'In fact, I did wonder at one stage yesterday if there were any more at home like him, but maybe a little older.'

'Did you really?' Mattie smiled.

'Really,' her mother confirmed. 'But that was before I realized the man was going to whisk my daughter off to Paris for the weekend!'

Now it was Mattie's turn to give a husky laugh. 'Oh, Mum. You don't think—' She broke off as the door opened after the briefest of knocks, her eyes widening in astonishment as she saw Jack standing there in the doorway.

He was dressed for the office, in dark suit, cream shirt and meticulously knotted brown tie, his hair still damp from an early-morning shower. And it must have been very early morning, because it was only eight o'clock now! Which also begged the question, what florist had he found open this time of the day from which to buy the bunch of spring daffodils he carried in his hand?

Mattie stood up slowly. 'What are you doing here?' she snapped impatiently, giving a pointed look in her mother's direction.

'Good morning to you too, Mattie,' Jack greeted cheerfully as he came fully into the kitchen and closed the door behind him. 'And I'm not actually here to see you,' he added, before turning to present her mother with the daffodils.

Well, really! Not only did he turn up here bearing gifts before she was even dressed—but he then proceeded to give those gifts to her mother!

'Why don't you go and get yourself ready for work?' Jack suggested. 'While I have a few quiet words with your mother,' he explained with a smile in Diana's direction.

Why didn't she—? Really, the man was insufferable. How dared he come here at this unsociable hour and start issuing orders? And, actually, unless she was mistaken, she was sure now those daffodils he had just given her mother had been picked from their own front garden!

She felt an absolute mess. Her hair wasn't even brushed, she had no make-up on, she was wearing her oldest—and most comfortable!—dressing-gown, over striped pyjamas. But, then, she hadn't been expecting visitors this time of the morning, had she?

'Please,' Jack added politely, just as Mattie was about to fire off a blistering reply.

'Better,' she snapped, picking up her unfinished mug of coffee to walk over to the doorway that led out to the hallway. 'Remember the ransom, Mum,' she couldn't resist adding.

Much to Jack's confusion, she was pleased to note as she left the room after giving him a triumphant grin.

What on earth was he doing here at this time of the morning? They had parted yesterday evening with an agreement to meet again this evening to discuss in more detail the arrangements for the weekend; Jack certainly hadn't mentioned anything then about coming here this morning. Mattie would have made at least a bit of an effort with her appearance if he had.

Not that it particularly mattered what she looked like; Jack didn't give the impression he found her in the least attractive, whatever she was wearing. She was just a means to an end for him. And she was the one who had better keep remembering that!

She took her time getting ready for work, taking a shower before putting on her make-up, dressing in a black business suit and pale cream blouse, and brushing her hair.

Quite a transformation, even if she did say so herself, Mattie decided admiringly as she studied her reflection in the full-length mirror on her wardrobe door. She looked what she was now, the proprietor of a successful greenery contract business and florist shop.

Unfortunately Jack wasn't there to appreciate her entrance as she swished back into the kitchen minutes later!

In fact, the kitchen was empty, not even her mother waiting there to tell her why Jack had wanted to speak to her. But, Mattie noted, the vase of daffodils had pride of place at the centre of the kitchen table...

Mattie finally tracked her mother down in the kennels'

office, sitting in the armchair with Sophie, the Yellow Labrador, resting her silky head on Diana's knee. The dog appeared ecstatic at this individual attention.

'Everything okay?' Mattie asked as her mother looked up and smiled at her.

'Fine,' her mother replied unconcernedly.

Mattie looked at her expectantly. After all, they didn't usually receive male visitors this early in the morning!

'Jack had to get to his office, but he said he would see you later this evening,' her mother told her.

And?

But again there was nothing else forthcoming, her mother continuing to stroke and pet Sophie for a while longer before standing up and moving to sit behind her desk.

By which time Mattie was chafing with impatience. What had Jack *wanted*?

Her mother glanced at her wrist-watch. 'Shouldn't you have left ten minutes ago?' she enquired.

'Mother!' Mattie exclaimed frustratedly.

Her mother raised innocent brows. 'Yes?'

Mattie glowered at her. 'Have you always been this irritating or is it only since the advent of Jack Beauchamp into our lives?'

Her mother laughed. 'You're so transparent, Mattie!' she chided affectionately. 'I couldn't resist teasing you a little.' She sobered. 'He just wanted to explain the situation to me and assure me that he doesn't have designs on my baby's virtue.'

'He doesn't?' Mattie frowned her consternation. 'I mean—of course he doesn't.' She spoke more forcefully. Although inwardly she felt more than a little annoyed that Jack had dared to discuss such a thing with her mother, of all people! 'But I had already told you that,' she added irritably.

Diana was soothing. 'Of course you had, but Jack just wanted to reassure me on that point.'

Jack… Her mother used his first name so casually, while Mattie, who was actually going away with him for the weekend, still felt very self-conscious about such familiarity.

Oh, well, no doubt by the time she returned from her weekend away with him she would be calling him several other names besides his first one. And none of them complimentary!

'Don't look so disappointed, Mattie,' her mother said ruefully.

'I'm sure that part of your agreement is negotiable!'

'Mum!' Her eyes widened protestingly.

'That's better.' her mother patted her hand. 'I always feel ancient when you call me "Mother" in that reproving tone,' she confided.

Considering her mother was only ten years or so Jack Beauchamp's senior, he would probably have been better off inviting her away with him for the weekend! Although Mattie found she didn't like the idea of that at all…

Despite all that she knew about him, four girlfriends etc., she was still attracted to the man. Which was a pretty dangerous thing to be when she was going to spend four days in Paris with him…

'What do you mean, you've told your family all about me?' Mattie stared across the dinner table at Jack. 'When did you tell them about me? What have you told them about me?' As far as she was aware, he didn't know anything about her!

Dinner with Jack Beauchamp was certainly an experience, she was learning. Not only had the *maître d'* greeted him by name as they'd entered the French restaurant where he had booked a table, but the proprietor had also come over and spoken to him once they had been seated next to the window that looked out over the London skyline. Jack had introduced her to the other man as his 'friend, Mattie Crawford'. With friends like Jack, she didn't need any enemies!

Jack shrugged unconcernedly. 'We all had lunch together today at my parents' house. And I simply told them that I would be bringing a Miss Mattie Crawford with me this weekend. What's Mattie short for, by the way?' he asked interestedly. 'Just in case anyone asks,' he added dryly.

Mattie wished he wouldn't turn his full attention on her in this way! Looking the way that he did, sophisticatedly handsome in a smart black suit, snowy white shirt and muted tie, it was rather unnerving to suddenly become the central focus of his attention.

At the same time, she also found his obvious closeness to his family extremely endearing. She couldn't think of too many single men in their early thirties who would want to bother. Given her own bond with her mother, at least this was one thing the two of them had in common.

'Matilda-May,' she muttered. 'How did someone with the name Jonathan end up being called Jack?' she added as a hasty diversion; she really hated having to own up to her full name. It was so old-fashioned for one thing, made her sound like someone's maiden aunt.

Well, the maiden part was right on the button, she

acknowledged sadly. After the disastrous mistake she had made with Richard, she had been extremely reluctant to accept so much as a date with another man during the last six months. Most men weren't too keen on being asked a lot of personal questions before you would even agree to go out with them! In fact, she couldn't remember the last time—apart from that drink with Jack yesterday evening—that she had been out at all.

She had brought out her trusty little-black-dress-to-suit-any-occasion for this evening. But as she looked around the room at the beautifully dressed women seated at the other tables in this exclusive restaurant, she knew she would have to take a serious look at her wardrobe before they left for Paris on Friday. The last thing she wanted was to look dowdy when she met Jack's family—

What did it matter what she looked like to Jack's family? It was very unlikely she would ever see any of them again after this weekend, anyway!

It mattered to her, came the instant response. She had no doubts that Jack's family were as wealthy as he was, that his sister and his mother would be wearing designer-label dresses to the engagement dinner on Saturday evening. Even if it took *all* of her savings to do it, Mattie was determined to buy herself a new dress for that.

'I was given the name Jonathan to distinguish me from my maternal grandfather, who had been christened John but was always called Jack,' Jack answered her question helpfully. 'And was promptly called Jack, anyway.'

It figured, Mattie thought. Families had a way of doing things like that. And talking of families...

'How many people will there be at this dinner party

on Saturday?' she asked, smiling shyly at the waiter as he delivered their first course of scallops with bacon and garlic. Mattie had ordered exactly the same meal as Jack, deciding to be guided by his choice; after all, he obviously ate in restaurants like this one all the time. This starter certainly smelt delicious.

'Including the two of us? Fifteen,' Jack replied casually.

Fifteen…!

Mattie's mouth dropped open in horror. She was expected to cope with fifteen—no, thirteen—complete strangers.

Ordinarily she had no problem meeting new people. After all, she did it on a day-to-day basis, and had done since she was extremely young. But these thirteen people were all Jack's family. Which was something else entirely.

'Don't worry about it.' Jack reached over and briefly squeezed her hand. 'After all, I'll be with you.' He grinned knowingly.

Because he knew damn well that didn't make her feel at all better about this coming weekend! How could it? He was enough of a torment on his own, without the rest of his family to cope with too.

'What are they like?' Mattie made an effort to look composed; she didn't have to appear quite such a country bumpkin!

'Try them and see,' he invited lightly, expertly spooning up one of the scallops from her plate and holding it poised in front of her mouth.

There was something rather—intimate, about having someone feed you in a restaurant, Mattie decided as she chewed briefly before swallowing down the mouth-watering food. Too intimate!

'I was actually referring to your family,' she bit out tautly, pointedly picking up her own cutlery to feed herself.

Jack's eyes widened, and then he smiled. 'Sorry. What are they like?' he repeated thoughtfully. 'Ordinary,' he finally responded. 'Like me.'

Mattie hated to tell him this, but there was nothing in the least ordinary about him!

'Well, none of them have two heads or twelve toes,' he amended humorously as he easily read the scepticism in Mattie's face.

'Ordinary, then,' she conceded. 'How many brothers and sisters do you—?'

'Did you check out your passport?' Jack interrupted with sudden urgency. 'The last thing I want is to turn up at the airport and find they won't let you on the plane because you don't have a valid passport.'

It sounded like a pretty good idea to Mattie! But, unfortunately, her passport was fine. So that was one get-out she could forget about!

'It's fine,' she assured him. 'But they may just have a little trouble at the airport when they see that the name on the ticket doesn't match the one in my passport,' she pointed out hopefully.

'Already taken care of,' Jack assured her. 'I telephoned the airline today and confirmed the ticket in your name.'

What he meant was, his secretary—the same secretary who ordered his bouquets of flowers by the quartet!—had called the airline and changed the name on the ticket.

She really must keep remembering that, Mattie chided herself. It was all too easy to become enslaved by the Beauchamp charm. So much so that she could almost believe they were going away to Paris just for a romantic weekend together. Almost...

'How efficient of you,' she rejoined with saccharine sweetness.

'Wasn't it?' Jack shot back with the same sugary insincerity. 'Have I told you how beautiful you look this evening, Mattie?' he said suddenly.

Once again Mattie found herself the focus of that charm he seemed to be able to turn on and off like a switch. It was lethal! Mattie now felt very hot, her heart beating a wild tattoo in her chest.

She gave him a scathing glance. 'Insincerity is the lowest form of flattery,' she told him hardly.

'But you do look wonderful,' Jack assured her softly. 'Your hair is the most amazing colour—what colour would you call that?' He looked admiringly at the heavy swathe of her layered hair as it fell past her shoulders.

'Blonde,' Mattie said tersely.

Jack shook his head, still looking at her hair. 'It's honey, and molasses, and yet there's also a hint of—'

'Salt and pepper?' she put in derisively. 'I think you're just hungry, Jack. I suggest you eat the rest of your scallops!'

He gave a laugh. 'It did sound rather like a recipe, didn't it?' he acknowledged.

For disaster! It was not a good idea for Jack to pay her compliments. It was an even worse idea for her to listen to them!

If only—

If only what?

If only she and Jack were out on a real date. If only she and Jack really were going to Paris for a romantic weekend.

If only!

But they weren't on a real date. They weren't going away for a romantic weekend; she was just a shield against the unwanted attentions of his future brother-in-law's sister. And it served her right if that was Jack's only interest in her!

How could a man like him possibly have any other sort of interest in her? She had been calling at his office building during the early evenings, twice a week, for the last year, and, although Jack had felt that he knew her when they'd met at her mother's boarding-kennels on Sunday, he certainly hadn't remembered where it was he might have seen her. Because in the ordinary course of events he just wouldn't notice someone like her. After all, it was what she was paid for, to be unobtrusive, to go about her work quietly and efficiently, to be virtually invisible.

Well, she had certainly made sure that was no longer the case where Jack was concerned, hadn't she?

'I realize that you're probably—practising, for this weekend, Jack,' she said stiltedly. 'But I really wish you wouldn't bother,' she added quickly as he would have spoken. 'I'm much more interested in knowing why you went to see my mother this morning?' she changed the subject abruptly.

Was it her imagination, or had his expression suddenly become guarded? Maybe, she accepted slowly. Although she had no idea why...

'Didn't she tell you?' Jack unhelpfully answered her question with one of his own.

'Well, of course she told me,' Mattie dismissed impatiently. 'I simply wondered—I wondered—'

'Mattie, you gave me the distinct impression last night that you didn't want your mother to be upset about your coming away with me this weekend—'

'I wonder why that was!' she said saucily.

Jack raised reproving brows. 'I merely wanted to assure Diana that—'

'You have no designs on her baby's virtue!' Mattie finished heatedly. 'You know, Jack, I really don't think—'

'Is that what your mother told you?' Jack cut in laughingly, those brown eyes once again filled with mirth.

Mattie became suddenly still, looking across at him with narrowed eyes. 'Yes, that's what she told me,' she said suspiciously. 'Isn't that what you said?'

'Amongst other things,' he dismissed vaguely. 'Anyway, she seemed much happier about the situation by the time I left her,' he finished confidently.

Mattie would have liked to pursue the subject of those other things, but unfortunately the wine waiter chose that moment to top up their glasses, and by the time he had left again Jack was obviously concentrating on enjoying his meal. She—

'You know,' he suddenly spoke up, 'your mother is still a very beautiful woman; has she never thought of marrying again?'

'Never,' Mattie answered unhesitantly, pleased at what he had said about her mother—even if, at the same time, she felt a twinge of jealousy too for the admiration he obviously felt.

Although it was an admiration Mattie shared, appreciating that it couldn't have been easy for her mother to be widowed at only twenty-three, to be left to bring up her three-year-old daughter on her own. So she shouldn't really complain if Jack also recognized what a beautiful and accomplished woman Diana was.

And yet...

Ridiculous. She had only met and spoken to the man because of his four girlfriends, and she hadn't felt in the least jealous concerning any of them; it seemed slightly ridiculous now to feel that way about her own parent.

'She must have loved your father very much?' Jack was looking at her speculatively.

'I believe so,' Mattie replied quietly. 'You still haven't told me what the travel arrangements are for Friday?' she prompted practically.

Jack continued to look at her for several long seconds, and then he appeared to physically relax. 'So I haven't,' he accepted lightly, then proceeding to do exactly that.

Mattie barely listened as he told her the time of the flight, the name of their hotel—although she did hear the part about it overlooking the Eiffel Tower—and the time they would be returning on Monday.

What was wrong with her?

She looked at Jack beneath lowered lashes as he continued to tell her the plans for the weekend, knowing as she did so that she liked everything about him: the way he looked, the way he dressed, his obvious closeness to his family, even his concern that her mother shouldn't be worried about her this weekend, and that he had personally gone to see her mother to reassure her. Mattie couldn't think of too many men who would have done that!

The only thing she didn't like about him was the thought of those four girlfriends.

The only thing!

Surely the fact that he had had four women in his life at the same time should tell her something else about him? Something such as, she would be an idiot to fall in love with him herself!

Except that she already knew it was going to prove very difficult for her not to, when she was spending four days with him in romantic Paris…!

CHAPTER FIVE

'WE'RE going for four days, Mattie, not four weeks!' Jack complained good-naturedly as he loaded her heavy suitcase into the back of his car on Friday morning.

Mattie didn't qualify his remark with an answer, merely gave him a lofty stare, having already noted his much smaller case in the boot.

She knew that she had probably overdone things with her clothes, but never having been to Paris before, in spring or any other time, she hadn't really known what the climate would be like, and she hadn't wanted to show her ignorance by asking Jack. Checking in the newspaper the last few days hadn't been much help either; yesterday it had rained in Paris, and the day before there had been sunshine. Very much like English weather, in fact.

So she had simply packed all the new clothes on which she had splashed out yesterday, along with everything else she already owned that she thought might be suitable.

'We women like to be prepared for any eventuality,' her mother was the one to laughingly answer Jack, having come outside to greet Harry, his Bearded Collie.

The dog was even now running excitedly between their legs, more like a puppy than six years old, his long grey and white coat freshly brushed, his eyes bright, his tail wagging happily. Obviously Harry hadn't realized yet that he was actually staying here.

Jack raised dark brows in Mattie's direction. 'Do you have the kitchen sink in there too?'

'And a spare bath plug,' she replied tauntingly.

'Now that just may come in handy.' He chuckled. 'I once stayed at a hotel where it took them two days to come up with a new bath plug because the last guest had stolen the original!'

'Well, if you will stay in these cheap places…!' Mattie derided, knowing full well that this man would only ever travel first class.

Jack grinned unconcernedly, looking extremely fit and handsome in black fitted trousers and a black shirt, a cream jacket lying on the back seat of his car.

Mattie hadn't known what she should wear to travel in either, finally deciding on her best pair of jeans, teamed with a white fitted tee shirt and black jacket. She looked smart, but comfortable, she had decided a short time ago when she'd checked her appearance in the mirror.

Whereas Jack looked exactly what he was: a wealthy sophisticate who had obviously done this dozens of times before.

Not with Mattie, he hadn't!

Her pulse had started beating a little faster just at the sight of him, the butterflies in her stomach telling of her inner excitement—or was it nervousness…? Whatever, it was the strangest sensation, shyness, and anticipation, mixed up with something that felt like fear, and yet wasn't. Very strange!

'Shall we take Harry round to his room and get him settled in?' Her mother briskly took charge of the situation. 'After all, you two will have to be on your way shortly,' she added practically.

Considering this was the first time Mattie had ever gone anywhere with a man, Mattie considered her mother was taking all of this very calmly. What exactly had Jack said when he'd come to see Diana the other morning? She certainly hadn't got a straight answer from him on Tuesday evening!

'Of course.' Jack's humour faded as he bent down to stroke his dog. 'Come on, boy, let's go and see what you make of this,' he said with a certain grimness.

He really wasn't happy about this, Mattie realized sympathetically. Although he really had nothing to worry about; her mother loved dogs, and they seemed to love her too.

'Why don't you wait here, Mattie?' her mother suggested now, a pointedly warning look in her eyes as she looked at Mattie over Jack's bent back.

'Of course,' Mattie instantly accepted; it was always difficult parting the owners from their pets, without having an audience.

Not that it did her too much good to have time to kick her heels while she waited for Jack; the more opportunity she had for thought, the more she thought this was a bad idea! In fact, she had picked up the phone several times over the last few days with the intention of telling Jack that. But each time she had remembered that she was the one who had created this difficulty for him, so it was up to her to help him out of it. If only she didn't feel quite so nervous!

Although she forgot all about that as Jack returned a few minutes later, his face pale, a nerve pulsing in his tightly clenched jaw.

Mattie stepped forward to touch his arm reassuringly. 'Harry really will be fine, you know,' she soothed gently.

Jack shook himself slightly, forcing a smile, although he was still very pale. 'Now I know how my parents felt every time they took me back to boarding-school!'

Mattie was sure it wasn't quite the same thing, but… 'And how did *you* feel once your parents had left to go home?'

His smile became happier. 'Oh, I laid it on thick before they left—tears, you name it—but within two minutes of them going out the door I was back amongst my friends, all of us talking at once as we discussed what pranks we could get up to the following term!'

'Well, I don't think Harry's quite doing that.' Mattie laughed at the thought. 'But I have no doubts that he's going to be just fine.' Her mother would make sure of it.

'He wasn't doing so badly when I left him,' Jack admitted as he opened the car door for her to get inside. 'He and Sophie were getting acquainted,' he explained at Mattie's questioning look.

'Don't worry.' Mattie shot him a mischievous look as he got in beside her. 'Sophie won't produce a brood of Yellow Labrador-Bearded Collie mix; she's had her tubes tied!'

'Well, really, Miss Crawford.' Jack pretended to look shocked. 'Isn't this a little early in our acquaintance to be discussing birth control!'

She could feel the heat that entered her cheeks. 'If we were really going away to Paris for a romantic weekend then I think this would be a little late to be discussing it!' she came back primly.

Jack burst out laughing, shaking his head as he sobered slightly. 'Do you have an answer for everything, Mattie Crawford?'

Not everything, no—unfortunately she had no answer at all to the way her heart leapt in her chest whenever he looked at her, let alone when he laughed in that completely uninhibited way!

But at least she had taken his mind off leaving Harry, which had been the intention, after all...

'Shouldn't we be on our way?' she prompted rather more sharply than she had intended, smiling slightly in an effort to take the sting out of her tone.

'Sure you've got everything?' he checked as he turned on the ignition.

Mattie gave the question exaggerated thought. 'I've only packed six pairs of shoes—do you think that will be enough—?' She broke off as he put the car in gear and accelerated down the driveway with such speed she felt as if she were pinned back against the seat. 'Oh, you do,' she went on sagely, settling herself more comfortably in the seat beside him.

Jack gave a snort. 'I thought sisters were bad enough, but girlfriends are—'

'I'm not your girlfriend,' Mattie reminded him frostily, perhaps a little more frostily than she intended, but she wanted to make sure the guidelines were clear before they left the country!

'For the next four days you are,' Jack returned unconcernedly. 'Jack and Mattie. Mattie and Jack. How do you think it sounds?' He quirked dark brows at her.

'Ridiculous,' she dismissed scathingly—while inside she could feel the warm glow evoked by hearing their names coupled together in that way. Which, in the circumstances, really *was* ridiculous!

'Please yourself.' He shrugged.

That was something she didn't think she would be

doing too much of in the next few days; her movements would be dictated by what Jack and his family were doing, not by what she personally might like to do. Which was a shame, because she really would have liked to see—

'I've booked a table for us for dinner this evening,' Jack interrupted her thoughts. 'But is there anywhere you would particularly like to go while we're in Paris?'

Her eyes widened. 'Me?'

'You,' he confirmed teasingly. 'I may be mistaken, but I have the feeling you've never been to Paris before.'

'Your feeling is correct,' Mattie admitted. 'But I thought this weekend was a family occasion?'

'I own up to being very close to my family, Mattie,' Jack answered evenly, 'but even I draw the line at spending the whole four days in their company when I could be alone with a beautiful woman, instead. Especially in Paris,' he added before Mattie could speak. 'We're meeting up with all of them tomorrow evening, but, other than that, our time's our own.'

Mattie had been struck dumb by his reference to 'a beautiful woman'—because he obviously meant her! But his next statement totally threw her.

'I quite fancy a day in Euro Disney myself,' Jack announced with a touch of self-derision. 'How about you?'

'Fine,' she replied vaguely, still reeling from learning they were to spend most of this weekend on their own together.

What on earth were they going to talk about for four days? And three evenings? And what about the nights…!

She swallowed hard. 'Jack—'

'Just relax, Mattie.' He reached over and squeezed her

hand with one of his, while keeping his other on the steering wheel and his eyes on the road. 'When did you last have a holiday?'

'A year ago,' she responded flatly.

'Then just think of this as a holiday. We're going to have fun, okay?'

'Okay,' she agreed.

He chuckled at her less-than-convinced tone. 'I was only joking when I made that reference to birth control, you know,' he teased. 'We have separate bedrooms at the hotel, honest!'

Well, that was something, at least. Although Mattie had a feeling, after she had spent all that time in Jack's undoubtedly seductive company, that she might be the one wishing that weren't the case...!

'So what do you think?' Jack prompted huskily as he came to stand behind her as she stood at the window of her hotel bedroom, his hands warm on her shoulders.

Mattie continued to gaze out at the Eiffel Tower, totally mesmerized. The sheer enormity of it, as it stretched skywards, was breathtakingly beautiful.

Jack hadn't been exaggerating when he'd said their hotel overlooked the Eiffel Tower; Mattie felt as if she could almost reach out and touch it!

'Mattie...?' Jack squeezed her shoulders.

'It's—I—' She shook her head. 'Thank you,' she finally managed through her emotion.

Jack slowly turned her to face him, looking down at her concernedly as he saw the unmistakable tears glistening in her eyes. 'For what?'

'For—for this.' The wave of her arms encompassed her hotel room as well as the magnificent view outside.

It was a beautifully large bedroom, its floral décor warmly welcoming. Mattie had kicked off her shoes once she was alone, her bare feet sinking into the thickness of the deep-rose-coloured carpet. There was a huge double bed dominating the room, and the *en suite* bathroom was the last thing in luxury, with its Jacuzzi bath and gold fittings. In fact, it was more luxurious than her own bedroom at home!

'You haven't seen all of it yet.' Jack grinned, taking her hand and leading her through the communicating door into the next room.

Mattie had assumed the room next to hers was Jack's bedroom—in fact, she had been slightly concerned by that open communicating door between the two rooms!—but that didn't prove to be the case.

If she had thought her bedroom luxurious, then the sitting-room she stood in was even more so: deep, luxurious armchairs, gleaming glass coffee-tables, bowls of fruit and flowers adorning their tops, a drinks cabinet discreetly in one corner of the room, a television in the other.

Although how anyone could possibly want to watch television when they could look out at the Eiffel Tower and its surrounding beauty, Mattie had no idea.

But if this was a sitting-room…?

'My bedroom is through here.' Jack seemed to read her confusion, moving forward to open the door beside the drinks cabinet, showing a bedroom identical in décor to Mattie's.

Although this one, she noticed, had twin beds rather than a king-size bed as in her own room…

Well, Jack had assured her they had separate bedrooms. He had just forgotten to mention that those bed-rooms were joined by a communal sitting-room!

'Come on, get some shoes on—one of the six pairs you mentioned earlier,' Jack urged dryly. 'And let's go out and explore!'

Mattie couldn't help but appreciate his enthusiasm, especially as she was sure that he must have been to Paris dozens of times before. But if he was willing to play the tourist for her sake, then she wasn't about to complain.

'Seeing all this through your eyes makes it all new to me too.' Once again Jack seemed able to read her thoughts, his arm moving lightly about her shoulders as he gave her a brief hug. 'Unless you would rather have something to eat first?' He frowned. 'Airplane food isn't very good, is it?' He grimaced.

Considering they had travelled first class, had been given drinks and nibbles in the lounge at the airport be-fore the flight and served a meal on board that could rival most restaurants, Mattie wasn't in the least hungry. And she told him so.

'I was hoping you would say that.' He grinned. 'Let's go out, hmm?'

His enthusiasm was infectious. Mattie was happy to put her shoes back on, deciding to leave her jacket in her room; the Paris weather—she was pleased to see!—was much like a warm, English summer day.

She hesitated once they were downstairs in the busy reception area of the hotel. 'Shouldn't you at least let your family know you've arrived?'

'I already have,' Jack responded. 'I called your mother too, by the way,' he added.

Her eyes widened at this. She had wanted to call her

mother earlier from her hotel room, just to let her know they had arrived safely, but, not speaking French, and having no idea how to dial out direct from her bedroom, she had deferred the call with the intention of asking for Jack's help later.

'That was very kind of you,' she said slowly.

'I needed to check on Harry, anyway.'

Of course he had. How silly of her to imagine it was anything else. 'How is he?' she asked politely.

'Fine,' he confirmed a little sheepishly. 'My family are all looking forward to meeting you tomorrow, by the way.'

Mattie swallowed hard, unable to reciprocate in the sentiment. It had all seemed much simpler when she'd been in England. Go to Paris with Jack, play the part expected of her, and then, at the end of the four days, return to her normal life.

Reality was something else entirely!

For one thing, travelling with Jack, and being accepted as his companion, had been an experience in itself. The hotel they were staying at was out of this world—well, out of Mattie's world. Also, the more time she spent in Jack's company, the more she liked being with him—perhaps too much?

In fact, her life in England, sharing a home with her mother, going off to work each day, fulfilling her office contracts in the evenings, was already starting to seem very far away. How was she going to feel after four days of this?

It was so easy to get caught up in the festive atmosphere around the Eiffel Tower, where there were street vendors, hundreds of other tourists strolling around or actually going up in the lifts to the top of the tower and lots more people just sitting down on the grassed area across the road relaxing in the sunshine.

'Time for a drink, I think,' Jack decided as he took in her slightly dazed expression, taking hold of her hand as they crossed the road and walked down the steps to one of the riverside cafés.

Still with Mattie's hand firmly held in his!

To anyone else, Mattie was sure, they just looked like another pair of lovers strolling in the sunshine, but the rapid beat of her heart, and the warmth in her cheeks, told her that she wasn't taking all of this in her stride.

The problem was, she realised as she watched Jack as he confidently ordered coffee for two in French, it would be all too easy to forget the real reason she was here. To just give herself up to the moment. To allow herself to be seduced by the romantic atmosphere. By Jack…!

But where would that leave her on Monday evening when they returned to England?

Heartbroken, came the instant response.

Jack was so much more than this charmingly indulgent companion. He was Jonathan Beauchamp, owner of JB Industries. He was the son of obviously wealthy parents—they had to be, if their daughter's engagement dinner was being held in Paris, of all places. Jack was also the man who, until four days ago, had not one, but four girlfriends.

And even if she managed to get past all those previous obstacles to there ever being a relationship between herself and Jack, Mattie had better not forget that last fact!

'Would you mind if we went back to the hotel?' she said abruptly. 'I'm feeling a little—travel-worn,' she added at his obviously disappointed expression. 'I would like to take a refreshing bath, maybe wash my hair, before we go out this evening.'

No doubt a bath would be refreshing, but what Mattie really wanted—desperately needed!—was time to herself so that she could build back her defences against falling for this man!

'Of course,' Jack accepted, drinking down his coffee. 'I should have thought of that earlier.' He threw some money down on the table to pay for their drinks. 'We don't have to do everything in one day, have a whole four days for you to fall in love with Paris,' he added with satisfaction.

She was already in love with Paris.

Just as she was very much afraid she was already in love with Jack Beauchamp!

CHAPTER SIX

DINNER on a river boat, cruising up the Seine, wasn't designed to bring Mattie to her senses when it came to her feelings for Jack!

When he'd told her earlier that he had booked a table for the two of them for dinner this evening, Mattie had assumed he'd meant at the hotel. But to her surprise, instead of going to the dining-room, Jack had walked them straight out of the foyer and into a taxi.

Ten minutes later they had arrived at the riverside, had been served a glass of champagne, before being shown to their table on board a luxurious river cruiser— and served another glass of champagne!

Mattie shook her head slightly dazedly. 'Jack, I don't think—'

'Paris is not the place for thinking, Mattie,' he laughed as he sat beside her, devastatingly attractive in a black dinner suit, snowy white shirt and black bow-tie, dark hair curling damply against his collar from the shower he had taken before coming out. 'It's the place to allow all your other senses full rein; to feel, taste, smell. But never allow yourself to get bogged down by thinking when in Paris, Mattie; it ruins the enjoyment of every-thing else!'

That was what was worrying her!

She had put on one of two new evening dresses this evening, a deep blue silk that exactly matched the colour of her eyes, its mandarin-style extremely flattering, the lower expanse of her tanned legs visible beneath its knee length, the three-inch heels of her new blue sandals giving her added height and elegance.

But, despite what Jack had said about not seeing any of his family until tomorrow evening, she had worn this dress with the assumption that they might perhaps see some of that family in the hotel dining-room this evening, having no idea that it would just be the two of them disappearing off somewhere on their own for dinner.

She wasn't sure it was a good idea for her to be quite this dressed up when she was having dinner alone with Jack.

Or for him to look so devastatingly attractive, either.

One of them seemed to have lost the plot here—and she was pretty sure it wasn't her!

'Maybe it does,' she conceded abruptly. 'But have you forgotten the reason I'm here?' She frowned.

'Hmm?' Jack turned from looking out the window beside them, lights from the boat playing along the riverside, illuminating all the wonders of Paris as they cruised slowly along.

'Jack!' she snapped frustratedly. 'The reason I'm here!' she reminded him.

'What about it?'

Mattie sighed her impatience with what she was sure was his deliberate obtuseness. 'How on earth is the two of us having dinner alone together on a river boat supposed to politely show this woman Sharon that you aren't interested in her?' she reasoned.

'I would have thought that was obvious,' Jack returned. 'The fact that we are having dinner alone together, on a river boat or anywhere else, must surely prove that I would rather be with you than with my family.'

Mattie couldn't deny that he had a point there. Although she was still far from convinced. Mainly, she knew, because she would rather have been somewhere else than alone with Jack, on a river boat or anywhere else!

'You didn't have to go to all this expense to do that; we could have just ordered room service or something,' she muttered awkwardly as their first course was delivered, a delicious *pâté de foie gras*.

Besides, if they had stayed at the hotel, Mattie knew she could have retreated to her bedroom, and Jack to his! Sitting in close proximity with him like this, his arm resting along the back of her chair, was doing absolutely nothing for her already disturbed senses!

'Don't be silly, Mattie,' Jack dismissed easily, straightening in his chair so that they could begin their meal. 'I didn't bring you to Paris to keep us both shut up in a hotel room.'

Mattie was beginning to wonder exactly what he had brought her to Paris for...

'Not unless it was in your bedroom, of course,' he turned to murmur huskily in her ear, his breath warm against her already sensitized flesh. 'After all, you do have the king-size bed,' he added throatily as Mattie turned wide eyes on him.

She turned sharply away, staring down at her plate of pâté, sure she would never be able to eat any of it; something seemed to have become lodged in her throat. Her heart, probably!

'Tell me, Mattie,' Jack continued conversationally beside her, calmly smoothing pâté onto a piece of warm toast. 'Just when did you decide there was a possibility I might try to have my wicked way with you while we're in Paris?'

She gasped, her eyes once again wide as she turned to look at him, incredulous. 'I—' She hesitated, chewing briefly on her bottom lip. 'I didn't—'

'Yes. You did.' Jack turned to smile at her. 'How about I make you a promise, Mattie?'

She swallowed hard before speaking. 'What sort of promise?'

He shrugged broad shoulders. 'I promise not to try to seduce you if you promise not to try to seduce me.'

Mattie was momentarily lost for words. 'I—I—I have no intention of trying to seduce you!' she finally managed indignantly.

'That's okay, then,' he responded, turning his attention back to his pâté.

While Mattie continued to stare at him. Really, the man was incredible, incorrigible! As if she would ever— as if she would ever what? Try to seduce him? Not intentionally, she acknowledged slowly. How did you seduce someone accidentally, Mattie? she instantly chided herself. Okay, she didn't intend seducing Jack Beauchamp in any way whatsoever!

Unless…

Unless what?

Unless she couldn't help herself!

She freely admitted that all of this was getting to her. The luxury of the hotel. The beauty of Paris. This romantic setting. Jack! Mainly Jack, she admitted with a sigh. He was just so—so—

'But if you do feel the urge, don't feel you have to hold it back, hmm?' he advised her.

Infuriating! Mattie concluded, shooting him an impatient glance, only to find him looking back at her with laughing brown eyes.

She wouldn't give him the satisfaction, she decided irritably. Even if she ached for him to kiss her, she would fight against the feeling. Even if—? She already ached for him to kiss her. And she *was* fighting against the feeling.

For all the good it was doing her!

Oh, how she wished she had never agreed to come here with Jack, that she were safely back at home in England, with her mother for company, and her work to keep her busy. She didn't—

She looked sharply at Jack as she realized he was chuckling softly. 'What's so funny?' she prompted suspiciously.

He sobered slightly. 'You are,' he answered. 'Despite what you obviously think, my love, I really don't have designs upon your gorgeous body.'

Mattie might have felt more convinced of that if he hadn't said, 'my love'. Not that she thought she was his love, it was just an endearment she could have done without.

Gorgeous body... She suddenly realized what else he had said. Did Jack really think she had a gorgeous body? Oh, help!

And she certainly needed all the help she could get as the meal, and the river cruise, progressed. All around them were other couples visibly deeply in love, completely wrapped up in each other as the romance of the evening cast its spell.

As it was casting its spell over Mattie...

How could it not, when, for all the notice anyone else

on board took of them, they might just as well have been alone, Jack's arm resting along the back of her seat when they weren't eating, often leaning close to her as he moved forward during the leisurely journey to point out a particular landmark?

By the time they left the boat it was almost midnight. The air was filled with the perfume of flowers and food. Mattie could only describe it as a seduction of the senses.

Jack hadn't needed to try to seduce her; she was fast losing the will to do anything but fall into his arms!

'I ordered the taxi to come back for us.' Jack pointed to the waiting car. 'But I think it might be nicer to walk back; what do you think?'

She thought that the sooner she put a stop to this evening, the better—safer!—it would be all round!

'That sounds lovely,' she heard herself reply.

She was unaccustomed to champagne, she decided; it had obviously addled her brain as well as her senses. She—

'I was hoping you would say that.' Jack grinned at her in the moonlight. 'I'll just tell the taxi driver about the change of plans. Don't go away,' he added huskily, squeezing her arm lightly before strolling over to the taxi.

Where could she go? Back to the hotel? What was the point of that when she was sharing a suite with Jack? Not back to the hotel, then? What was the point of that, either? She would have to go back there some time, if only to collect her things. To the airport? Dressed like this, her money, credit cards and—more importantly— her passport, still in her hotel room, she wasn't going to get very far.

'Sorry to keep you waiting,' Jack apologized as he rejoined her on the quayside, the warmth of his smile in those dark brown eyes.

As Mattie looked at him she knew she had been waiting for this man all her life!

The knowledge hit her with the force of a sledgehammer. Taking her breath away. Leaving her weak at the knees. The colour flooding and then as quickly fading from her cheeks.

'Hey, are you okay?' Jack asked, reaching out to clasp her arms as he looked down at her quizzically.

Mattie wasn't sure she would ever be okay again. This had to be the most irresponsible, the most stupid thing she had ever done in her life. Jack Beauchamp. Of all men!

'Mattie…?' he pressed concernedly at her lack of reply.

She swallowed hard, giving a slight shake of her head. The last thing she wanted—needed!—was for Jack to even guess how she felt. That would be just too humiliating!

'Of course I'm okay,' she finally answered, determined to put an end to this. 'And, despite what you may have said earlier, I'm curious as to what usually happens now.'

'Sorry?' He frowned his confusion.

'Oh, come on, Jack.' She forced herself to laugh derisively. 'It's pretty obvious you've done all this before, so what happens next?'

His hands fell away from her arms, his gaze watchful now. 'I'm not sure I understand what you mean.'

'Seduction, Jack,' she returned scathingly. 'We've had the romantic dinner for two.' She indicated the boat behind them. 'Paris has obviously worked its charm. We're about to take a romantic stroll in the moonlight; what comes next?'

His gaze narrowed. 'You're under the impression that I make a habit of bringing women to Paris and wining and dining them into submission?'

Mattie deliberately ignored the warning in his tone and expression; she had to put distance between them. For her own sake!

'It does seem rather an expensive method of seduction,' she acknowledged mischievously. 'But one hundred-per-cent foolproof, I would have thought.' She quirked mocking brows as she smiled at him knowingly.

There was no answering warmth in those dark brown eyes, his mouth a thin, uncompromising line. 'What comes next, Mattie,' he rasped abruptly, 'is we walk back to the hotel, say goodnight, and then go to our respective bedrooms!'

'Jack, you aren't annoyed with me for seeing through all this, are you?' she teased. 'After all, the only reason I'm here at all is because I messed up your relationships with four other women, one of whom was originally meant to accompany you this weekend,' she reminded him. And she had better keep remembering that, herself!

'After the promise I made you earlier, is that really what you think has been happening this evening?' he responded hardly.

She nodded. 'Not that I don't appreciate all this.' She fleetingly indicated their romantic surroundings. 'But, honestly, it's completely wasted on me,' she added with a lightness she was far from feeling.

'Obviously,' he bit out tersely.

'You *are* annoyed that I wasn't taken in by all this!'

'Not at all,' Jack drawled, visibly relaxing. 'But you can't blame a man for trying!'

Possibly not, Mattie inwardly conceded. It was the fact that he had succeeded that bothered her!

'Shall we go?' Jack held out his arm for her to take.

Mattie hesitated only slightly before slipping her hand into the crook of his arm, just touching him was enough to make her tremble all over again. But not to take his arm would give the impression she wasn't as controlled as she appeared. And the last thing she wanted was for Jack to guess that his roundabout method of seduction had succeeded!

None of this evening had been wasted on her, she acknowledged miserably as they walked briskly back to their hotel; in fact, it had been all too successful, but probably not in a way that Jack could even begin to guess.

She was in love with the man. She loved the way he looked, the way he talked, his sense of humour, his closeness to his family, even his affection for his dog! In fact, the only thing she didn't love about him was the fact that he obviously enjoyed the company of women so much that he had had four girlfriends at the same time.

That 'only thing' again…!

As far as Mattie was concerned, it had to be the most important thing. It wasn't just Richard's subterfuge the previous year that made her feel this way. She also had the example of her parents' short but happy marriage, her mother's devotion for the last twenty years to the memory of her dead husband; anything but a one-to-one relationship was completely out of the question for

Mattie. Something she already knew, from Jack's past behaviour, she would never be able to have with him.

Which meant she couldn't have any sort of relationship with him at all.

Devastating, but true.

Even more devastating when she reviewed the evidence of other couples strolling along hand in hand beside the river and near the Eiffel Tower, the structure all lit up now, its golden glow filling the night sky.

But neither she nor Jack had spoken as they walked back to the hotel, a definite distance between them now, despite Mattie's hand still resting in the crook of his arm.

By the time they reached the hotel Mattie felt completely miserable.

What was wrong with her, for goodness' sake? She had decided that she had to end the intimacy that had developed between Jack and herself throughout the evening, had known that for her own peace of mind she *had* to do that. Now that she had done it, why was she so unhappy?

Because she wanted to throw caution to the wind, wanted to give herself up to the moment, to lose herself in Jack's arms, not to think too deeply, especially about tomorrow.

She turned to him as they travelled up in the lift together. 'Jack—'

'Mattie— Sorry.' He grimaced as they both began talking at once. 'Ladies first,' he invited lightly.

The lift had come to a halt, the two of them stepping out into the carpeted corridor.

Mattie looked up to meet his searching gaze. 'I just—I—'

'Mattie, if I don't soon kiss you…!' Jack groaned before his head lowered and his mouth took warm possession of hers.

All her earlier objections, all caution, deserted her as she responded to that kiss, her arms up about Jack's shoulders as she clung to him, knowing this was where she had wanted to be all evening.

Their bodies moulded perfectly together as that searching kiss continued, Mattie's breasts aching with desire, all of her body feeling as if it were on fire with—

'Jack! Oh, Jack, thank goodness you're back!'

Mattie pulled sharply out of Jack's arms at the first sound of that female voice. She hadn't been aware earlier of anyone else in the carpeted corridor that led to their suite, but as she saw a figure now running down the corridor towards Jack she realized the other woman must have been standing in the doorway of their suite all along. Waiting for Jack.

Mattie took in the other woman's appearance at a glance. She was beautiful: tall, with flowing blonde hair, her features exquisitely lovely, with a figure to match.

And Mattie could only stand by and watch as, a sob catching in the woman's throat, she launched herself into Jack's arms.

'Tina!' Jack recognized instantly. 'What is it?' he prompted worriedly. 'What's wrong?'

Tina!

Mattie had no idea what the other woman was doing here, but she had no difficulty in recognizing Tina as one of the names that had accompanied those four bouquets she had delivered—wrongly!—on Saturday!

Which meant that Tina was probably the woman who should have been here with Jack this weekend…

'It's Jim,' the woman looked up to choke emotionally, her beautiful face streaked with tears. 'I—I've left him!'

'You've done what?' Jack rasped disbelievingly, holding the woman at arms' length now.

Tina's head went back defensively. 'I've left Jim,' she repeated determinedly.

The *married* woman who should have been here with Jack this weekend, Mattie realized heavily.

Jack shook his head dazedly. 'You can't have done.' He shook his head.

'But I have,' the woman said firmly, quickly gaining control, the tears held firmly in check now, too.

Mattie had the distinct feeling that she shouldn't be here. In fact, it was much more than a feeling—she didn't want to be here! 'Jack.' She reached out and touched his arm, the fazed look on his face as he turned to look at her telling her that, for the moment, despite their earlier closeness, he had forgotten she was still there. 'I think it would be better if I left the two of you alone to talk,' Mattie told him stiltedly.

'I— Yes.' He still looked totally stunned. 'Perhaps that would be best. I—' He shook his head, clearly totally disoriented by the other woman's arrival. 'I need time to sort out this situation,' he added apologetically.

Mattie didn't need to be told twice, holding back her own tears as she walked quickly away from the other couple, relieved when she reached the sanctity of her own bedroom and closed the door behind her.

She threw herself down on the bed, pulling the pillow over her head so that she shouldn't hear Jack and the beautiful Tina when—if—they came into the suite.

This was awful. So much more awful than anything else that had ever happened to her.

It was pretty obvious that Tina was the woman who should have accompanied Jack to Paris, before those plans had fallen through—with or without Mattie's deliberate mistake over the flowers...? It didn't really matter; Tina was here now. Not only was she here, she seemed to have walked out on her husband as well.

Which left Mattie precisely where?

CHAPTER SEVEN

'MATTIE? Mattie! Are you awake?' A second knock on her bedroom door accompanied this last question.

Of course she was awake. Awake and miserable. And she didn't think letting Jack into her bedroom at this late hour—a quick glance at the glowing digital bedside clock showed her it was two-thirty in the morning!—was going to do anything to alleviate that misery. Thank goodness she had thought to lock the connecting door to her bedroom after getting ready for bed!

'Mattie?' he called again urgently. 'I really do need to talk to you.'

She would just bet he did! Well, it could wait until later when all he intended doing was explaining to her that, now Tina was here after all, she might as well return to England!

'Mattie…?' he urged frustratedly.

Go away, she pleaded under her breath. Just go away and leave me alone.

Maybe later she would be better able to deal with this. Although she wouldn't count on it!

Not that it was exactly Jack's fault that Tina had turned up in Paris after all, but that didn't make Mattie feel any better. Or any more kindly towards Jack. If his life hadn't been such a complicated mess in the first place then none of this would have happened.

She wouldn't have met and fallen in love with him, either!

What an idiot, she groaned self-derisively.

The situation was made all the worse, as far as Mattie was concerned, because of that kiss the two of them had shared before they'd been so rudely interrupted! In fact, if Tina hadn't announced her presence in that dramatic way, Mattie knew she would have told Jack she had changed her mind about the whole seduction.

Double the idiot, she inwardly remonstrated with herself.

Luckily, she hadn't actually got around to telling him that before the other woman had interrupted them, but a few seconds later and she would have done!

She curled up into a ball of misery, willing Jack to go away from her bedroom door now.

'Mattie, let me in, hmm?' he encouraged softly. 'We really do need to talk. I know how it must have looked to you earlier, and I—I need to explain.'

Explain what? That bringing her here had been a mistake? That the kiss they had shared had been a mistake too? That he would put the situation right by booking her on a plane back to England as soon as possible?

Well, he needn't bother; she was quite capable of booking her own ticket and taking herself back home!

It took every ounce of her will-power not to call out and tell him exactly that. But Tina's arrival had totally unnerved her, and she wasn't emotionally strong enough yet to tell Jack exactly what she thought of him.

Later this morning she would be, though!

'Okay.' Jack's sigh could be heard through the thickness of the bedroom door. 'But I do intend talking to you, Mattie. I need to explain. To—oh, to hell with this!' he bit out impatiently. 'I can't talk to you through a locked door! I'll talk to you later,' he muttered before moving away.

Maybe he would. And maybe he wouldn't. It all depended on when Mattie could manage to get a flight back to England!

Because she *was* going home today. Come rain, shine, Jack Beauchamp, she was going home, should never have agreed to come here in the first place.

She rolled over in the bed, glancing across the room to where her suitcase was already packed and waiting for her departure. All she had to do was get through these early hours.

All!

She had no idea a few hours could seem so long, finally getting up at six o'clock, dressing in jeans, tee shirt and jacket, checking that the rest of the suite was in silence, before quietly letting herself out of the bedroom.

Paris, at six-thirty on a Saturday morning, was as deserted as anywhere else would be at this early hour, with the odd late night reveller making their way home. But, other than that, it was just Mattie sitting on a bench, with a few pigeons at her feet.

'Sorry, I don't have any food for you,' she told them apologetically as they pecked around hopefully on the pavement.

She had thought she cared for Richard, but now recognized it had been her pride that had been hurt in that particular situation. How did she know? Because now she really was in love. With Jack. And it was the most painful feeling of her entire existence!

Where was the gladness? The happiness? The wonderful euphoria she had always thought went with falling in love?

But, she realized, it was *whom* she had fallen in love with, that was the problem!

Jack Beauchamp.

Caring son and brother? Or womaniser?

For a while last night Mattie had thought the former, but the arrival of his married lover implied he was definitely the latter.

But she loved him, anyway. It was ridiculous, and yet—

'Hello, there; I didn't think I would find anyone else up and about this time of the morning,' came a British voice.

Mattie had been so lost in thought that she hadn't noticed there was anyone else around, forcing herself to smile as the older woman came to sit next to her on the bench-seat next to the Eiffel Tower.

'Good morning,' she greeted huskily.

The older woman returned her smile ruefully. 'I thought you had to be English; mad dogs and Englishwomen stay out early in the morning,' she misquoted.

Mattie laughed softly, instinctively liking the other woman; she was probably aged in her late sixties, with neatly permed grey hair, her blue eyes kind in her lined face, with a cuddly grandmotherly figure.

Instinctively liked her?

Mattie's smile faded. Where had that instinct got her so far? In love with completely the wrong man was where! This woman beside her could be a mass murderer for all the good her instinct had done her the last few days!

'Although I must say, my dear,' the older woman continued kindly, 'you seem a little young to be suffering from insomnia.'

Mattie shrugged. 'I was just taking a last look round before returning to England later today.' At least, she hoped she would be able to return later today.

'Oh, what a shame,' the other woman sympathized. 'And have you enjoyed your stay? But of course you have; how could you not have enjoyed Paris?' she answered her own question.

Which was just as well—because Mattie's own answer would have been quite different!

The woman smiled. 'I first came to Paris thirty-five years ago for my honeymoon,' she explained wistfully. 'It seems like only yesterday to me,' she continued. 'Although I don't think my five children and three grandchildren would agree, do you?' she added laughingly.

'Paris is very romantic.' Mattie spoke slowly, choosing her words carefully.

The woman looked at her quizzically. 'Are you here with your young man?'

Mattie very much doubted Jack could be called anyone's young man; he was much too free with his charms to ever be that exclusive.

'No,' she answered flatly. 'I—no, not really. It just hasn't been a very—successful visit.'

'What a shame.' The woman smiled sadly. 'I'm here for a family party. My youngest daughter's engagement dinner,' she confided warmly.

Alarm bells had begun to go off inside Mattie's head at the mention of a family party, but that it was her youngest daughter's engagement dinner was just too much of a coincidence.

This woman had to be Jack's mother!

Could things get any worse? She had thought not, but they certainly seemed to have done so in the last few minutes.

She looked at the woman beside her with new eyes, looking for any likeness to Jack in the small stature and kindly lined face, and finding none. Jack must take after his father, then, because Mattie couldn't believe there could possibly be two English families in Paris this weekend celebrating the engagement of the youngest daughter.

'I think I had better be going,' Mattie said awkwardly, standing up. 'I— It's been nice speaking to you. I hope your party is a success this evening,' she added sincerely.

'Thank you, my dear.' The other woman smiled up at her.

Mattie turned away, her feet feeling leaden, her heart even heavier.

'I was so hoping you would be able to join us, Mattie. It is Mattie, isn't it?'

Mattie had spun round at the first sound of her name, staring at the older woman with horrified eyes now. It was bad enough that she had inadvertently spoken to Jack's mother in the first place, but doubly awful that the other woman obviously knew exactly who she was, too.

Which begged the question: how had this lady guessed who she was?

'Do come and sit down again, Mattie,' Jack's mother invited warmly, patting the wooden seat beside her. 'I'm Betty Beauchamp, by the way,' she introduced herself as Mattie moved like an automaton to obey the invitation.

She dropped down heavily onto the seat beside the older woman, still staring at her with bewildered eyes. 'I—Mattie Crawford,' she reciprocated haltingly.

'Don't look so worried, Mattie—I may call you Mattie, I hope? I'm not psychic or anything. I just happened to see you and Jack leaving the hotel together yesterday evening,' she explained.

Whereas Mattie hadn't been aware of anyone else but Jack the previous evening...

'I see,' Mattie accepted warily, still not sure what she could say to Mrs Beauchamp. Without offending her!

Betty looked sad. 'I have no idea what Jack has done to upset you, my dear, but it's obvious, this morning, that he has done something. Which is a pity, because the two of you looked so happy together last night.' She shook her head.

That was before Tina's arrival. Before Mattie had realized she was now completely superfluous to this weekend.

But as Mattie had no idea just how much Betty knew about her arrangement with Jack for this weekend, she wasn't quite sure how to answer her. And so she decided not to answer at all.

Betty sighed. 'Edward and I were so pleased when Jack rang us on Wednesday evening and told us he was bringing a young lady with him this weekend—'

'On Wednesday?' Mattie echoed sharply now. 'But I—Wasn't Jack always bringing a—a young lady with him?'

'Oh, no,' Betty dismissed indulgently. 'This is the first time Jack has ever introduced us to any of his—friends.

Which is why we were so hopeful—Jack is very protective of his private life as a rule.'

In the circumstances, that wasn't surprising!

Nevertheless, Mattie was still puzzled by the other woman's disclosure. 'But surely Jack *was* bringing someone with him this weekend...?' she persisted.

'Not until Wednesday, no.' His mother shook her head confidently. 'As I said, Edward and I were so excited at the prospect of meeting you.' She smiled warmly.

Mattie's own smile came out as more of a grimace. Because she didn't understand this conversation at all. Jack had assured her that her deliberate mismanagement of the cards on the flowers she had delivered for him had messed up his relationships—

But had he?

She tried to remember back to that conversation they had had, to remember exactly who had said what, but it was difficult as Betty spoke again.

'I know Jack can sometimes be a little—forceful, in his ways.' She looked slightly embarrassed. 'He gets that from his father, I'm afraid. I've learnt to deal with it, of course, but then I've had years of experience,' she continued indulgently. 'But Jack can be such a thoughtful boy, too, that the family usually overlooks any—little faults, he may have.'

Mattie's head was buzzing as a number of possibilities suddenly came to mind. 'Tell me, Mrs Beauchamp—'

'Betty, please,' the other woman invited lightly.

'Tell me, Betty,' Mattie began slowly, 'if Jack is so thoughtful, why does he never send you flowers?' The other woman looked taken aback by the strangeness of the question. As well she might, Mattie inwardly acknowledged, but the way in which Betty answered it was very important to her.

'Why, how clever of you to know that!' she exclaimed. 'Jack knows I have an aversion to cut flowers— I believe they should remain in the ground to be enjoyed rather than brought into the house to die. And so, whenever Jack sends flowers to the girls, he always buys me a rose-bush to plant in the garden, instead. I believe I have at least fifty by now,' she added with satisfaction.

'Girls?' Mattie repeated, a slight edge to her voice now. Although she had a feeling she already knew the answer to this particular question. If she was right, she was going to throttle Jack when next she saw him!

'My four daughters,' Betty told her proudly. 'I did tell you that I have five children? Jack is the eldest, of course, followed by Christina, then the twins, Sarah and Caroline, and lastly—'

'Alexandra,' Mattie finished rather more forcefully than she intended. But if what she thought were true—! 'She would be Sandy?' she probed evenly.

'Yes,' Betty confirmed, frowning slightly. 'Of course, this will be Sandy's second marriage, but the first one was such a disaster that we're all just very pleased to be celebrating her second chance at happiness.'

Mattie wasn't sure she wanted to hear a potted version of the Beauchamp family history! Although this explanation did help to explain away Sandy's surname on the flowers Jack had sent. And talking of flowers...

'Your other daughters would be Tina, Sally, and Cally?' she pressed.

'Families are terrible for nicknames, aren't they?'

Play The *Lucky Hearts* Game

and get...
FREE BOOKS & a FREE GIFT...
YOURS to KEEP!

Yes! I have scratched off the silver card. Please send me my **FREE BOOKS** and **FREE MYSTERY GIFT**. I understand that I am under no obligation to purchase any books as explained on the back of this card. I am over 18 years of age.

Scratch Here!
then look below to see what you can claim...

P3JI

Mrs/Miss/Ms/Mr .... Initials ....

BLOCK CAPITALS PLEASE

Surname ....

Address ....

....

.... Postcode ....

Twenty-one gets you
4 FREE BOOKS and a
MYSTERY GIFT!

Twenty gets you
1 FREE BOOK and a
MYSTERY GIFT!

Nineteen gets you
1 FREE BOOK!

TRY AGAIN!

NO STAMP NEEDED!

THE READER SERVICE™
FREE BOOK OFFER
FREEPOST CN81
CROYDON
CR9 3WZ

NO STAMP
NECESSARY
IF POSTED IN
THE U.K. OR N.I.

Betty pondered affectionately. 'Of course, Jack is really Jonathan, too, but we've always called him Jack.'

No doubt about it, Mattie *was* going to kill him!

Those four women, the ones she had assumed were the women in Jack's life, were all his sisters!

Incredible. Amazing. Absolutely unbelievable!

It didn't matter at that moment that Jack had tried to tell her he didn't have four girlfriends, he had still talked her into—blackmailed her into!—coming away with him this weekend under false pretences. Why, she had no idea. What she did know was that he was a lying, conniving, double-talking, blackmailing—!

At the moment Mattie was too angry to think of any more expletives she could hurl at him. But no doubt by the time she saw him again she would have thought of a few more. Because she no longer intended leaving today, after all.

Jack had lied about needing her to replace the original woman he'd intended bringing here in an effort to avert Sharon's attention—because he had never intended bringing a woman here with him in the first place.

For some reason—as yet unknown!—he had brought her to Paris under false pretences, and in her eyes that made him just as guilty as she had initially been concerning those cards on the flowers. It would be interesting to see how *he* liked having to pretend in front of his family that everything in his world was hunky-dory—knowing as Mattie now did their hopes about this relationship!

'Would you excuse me—Betty?' Mattie added her name awkwardly, and stood up. 'I think I would like to go back to the hotel now. I think perhaps Jack and I can

sort out this little problem, after all,' she declared decisively.

'Oh, I do hope so.' His mother beamed. 'The family
is so looking forward to meeting you.'

Again Mattie felt that twinge of guilt. But Jack was
the one who should feel guilty, not her, she instantly
told herself; if his mother was anything to go by, then
his family were delightful, and he had no right deceiving
them in this way. For whatever reason.

'But I'm afraid you won't find Jack back at the hotel
just now,' Betty explained. 'He's gone to the airport to
meet my eldest daughter's husband,' she added with a
frown. 'As you know, Tina arrived here last night de-
claring she had left Jim. She has always been hotheaded,
I'm afraid.' Betty shook her head. 'But this time she's
gone too far. And Jim is such a nice young man.'

So Jack had gone to the airport to meet his brother-
in-law, had he? Which was why the suite had been so
quiet when she'd left earlier. It was probably also the
reason Jack had been so desperate to talk to her at two-
thirty this morning; he had wanted to sort out this situation between them before Mattie could do a disappearing act while he was away at the airport, and so leave
him with egg on his face where his family were concerned.

Well, he no longer needed to worry about that happening; Mattie didn't intend going anywhere but back to
the hotel.

What Jack did have to worry about, though, was how
Mattie was going to behave for the rest of this weekend.
Because if Jack had enjoyed making a fool of her the
last few days, then it was time he learnt exactly what it
felt like to be on the receiving end!

'I'm sure they will work things out,' Mattie assured Betty Beauchamp. 'After all, this is Paris,' she encouraged as the older woman still looked doubtful.

'So it is.' Betty brightened. 'And I'm so glad you've changed your mind about leaving.'

Mattie felt another prick of conscience at the other woman's genuine pleasure in her decision to stay on, after all. But, she instantly reasoned, Jack was the one who should have the guilty conscience. The fact that she now knew the real identity of the recipients of the flowers Jack sent to those four women made no difference to the fact that he had always intended passing her off to his family as his girlfriend. And considering, as Mattie now knew, he had never brought even one of his friends to meet his family before, he should have known exactly what conclusion they would all come to.

The only thing that had really changed was that Mattie now knew the truth about those four women in his life…

'Er—perhaps it would be better, Betty, if neither of us mentioned this particular conversation to Jack?' Mattie looked at the older woman. 'I'll tell him the two of us have met, of course, but I don't think he would like the idea of the two of us—discussing him in this way.'

'I'm sure he wouldn't,' Betty agreed instantly, obviously relieved at the suggestion. 'It was just that when I saw you leaving the hotel earlier I couldn't resist coming and talking to you. And I'm so glad I did.' She smiled. 'I shall very much look forward to seeing you again this evening,' she finished.

'Thank you,' Mattie said, before turning and walking slowly back to the hotel.

What on earth did Jack think he was doing? Okay, so

Mattie accepted he found the attentions of his future brother-in-law's sister a pain in the— He had wanted to put this Sharon off without offending anyone. But what on earth had he imagined the rest of his family were going to think about him bringing a 'girlfriend' with him this weekend, especially as he had never done such a thing before?

Exactly what Betty Beauchamp obviously thought: that Jack was actually serious about her.

She could only conclude that Jack hadn't thought about that side of things at all, had just seen a way to rid himself of Sharon's unwanted attentions—while at the same time have a little fun at Mattie's expense.

Well, they would just see later today who was having fun and who wasn't!

CHAPTER EIGHT

'MATTIE, I— What are you doing?'

Mattie almost laughed out loud at the stunned look on Jack's face as she launched herself into his arms, her face raised expectantly for his kiss.

She looked pointedly into the sitting-room behind him, instantly stepping back. 'I thought I had better show some affection, in case we weren't alone,' she said— knowing very well that they were. But Jack couldn't possibly know that she had looked into the sitting-room a few minutes ago when she'd heard him arrive back from the airport and already knew they were by themselves!

Jack glowered darkly. 'Very commendable, I'm sure.' He ran a hand tiredly through the dark thickness of his hair. 'If a little misguided. I'm hot, sticky, and tired,' he explained at her raised brows.

Actually, he looked absolutely shattered; perhaps trying to sort out the situation between his eldest sister and her husband had taken its toll!

But Mattie was in no mood to feel in the least sorry for him. 'Hardly in the mood for love, hmm?' she teased, blue eyes glowing mischievously.

But not too mischievously, she hoped; she didn't want Jack to realize this early in the day that she was completely aware of the game he had been playing with her. No…she certainly didn't want him to realize that yet…

'Would you like me to order you some lunch while

you take a shower and freshen up?' she offered, knowing by his quizzical expression that, after the way they had parted last night, he was totally confused by her friendly behaviour. Which was exactly what Mattie wanted him to be. It would serve him right if he were to think, after the intimacy of the evening they had spent together yesterday, that she was taking this whole thing seriously.

Which was how, during the hours when she'd waited for him to return from the airport, she had decided to play it. Given what she now knew, it would probably frighten the life out of Jack if he believed she was really falling for him.

'I got your message, by the way,' she informed him casually, having been handed a letter by Reception when she'd returned to the hotel after her walk early this morning. It hadn't been a very long message: 'Gone to the airport. Don't do anything until I get back. Jack.'

Don't do anything until he got back…! What did he think she was, an obedient pet as blindly devoted to him as Harry was? Because if that was what he thought—

'So I see,' Jack drawled at the obvious fact she was still here. 'You—'

'Would you like some lunch?' Mattie pointedly picked up the telephone receiver. 'I ordered a club sandwich earlier; it was delicious,' she elaborated encouragingly.

'A club sandwich will be fine,' Jack accepted, still looking confused by her obvious friendliness.

After the way they had parted the evening before, after the conclusions Jack must believe Mattie to have come to concerning Tina's arrival—in view of his deception to Mattie about who Tina actually was!—perhaps that wasn't so surprising.

But Mattie had barely started yet!

'By the way, I met your mother earlier,' she told him lightly, sitting down in one of the armchairs, telephone to her ear as she put through her call to Room Service, holding back a smile as she saw the start of surprise on Jack's face that he was unable to hide successfully. Surprise that was quickly followed by a guarded wariness.

'My mother?' he repeated. 'But—'

'Room Service?' she answered the person who had just answered her call. 'One club sandwich, please,' she requested politely, putting her hand over the receiver to speak to Jack. 'Would you like something to drink with that?' she prompted brightly.

'A pot of strong coffee, I think,' he answered, still looking warily at Mattie.

She ordered the coffee, giving the room number, before ringing off and standing up to glance at her wristwatch. 'I have to go now, I'm afraid,' she told him regretfully. 'I've booked the full works at the beauty salon downstairs this afternoon,' she informed him helpfully. 'I want to look my best for this evening.'

Jack looked more puzzled than ever. 'Mattie—'

'If I were you, Jack—' Mattie picked up her shoulder bag in preparation of leaving '—I would take a nap after you've eaten lunch; you're looking rather haggard.'

'Whereas you look bright and cheerful,' he muttered disgruntledly, obviously less than amused by her blunt observation.

'Why shouldn't I?' Mattie mused brightly and cheerfully—deliberately ignoring the way his face had darkened ominously. 'We're in Paris, I'm spending the afternoon being pampered at a beauty salon, we're going out to dinner at the Eiffel Tower this evening; what could be more perfect?'

He gave a heavy frown. 'But last night—'

'I'm sure you've managed to deal with last night,' she cut in dismissively. 'And, after all, it is me your family is expecting to meet this evening, isn't it?' she reminded him. 'Now I really do have to go, Jack.' She gave another glance at her wrist-watch before hurrying over to the door. 'Your mother is delightful, by the way,' she added truthfully before letting herself out of the suite.

Ha!

Now who was disconcerted? she thought triumphantly as she went down in the lift. Let them just see how Jack liked being left completely in the dark about what was actually going on. Mattie doubted he was going to like it any better than she had!

Having deliberately booked herself into the hotel's beauty salon this afternoon, as a way of avoiding answering any of the questions she knew Jack must be dying to ask her, she was determined to enjoy the experience of just sitting back and relaxing as the stylist trimmed and styled her hair, then a face-pack, before a light make-up was applied, and her nails manicured and lacquered. It was rather soothing to just let her mind drift, to feel completely pampered in this way.

Don't get too used to it, she instructed herself as she sat and had her nails painted. It was back to work and normality on Tuesday morning.

A normality that in no way included Jack Beauchamp, she acknowledged heavily, some of her earlier satisfaction fading at this reality. Because, despite everything, Mattie knew she was in love with the man.

He was infuriating, puzzling, enigmatic. But she loved him anyway. Quite what she was going to do about—

Her thoughts came to an abrupt halt as she unwittingly heard part of the conversation from the next booth.

'Mum and Dad are absolutely thrilled about Tina's pregnancy,' the woman spoke confidingly.

'So is Tina,' another woman replied excitedly. 'She just expected Jim to do and say a little more, after she had told him the good news, than announce that he guessed the skiing holiday was off for this Christmas! But that's just Jim's sense of humour, and Tina will realize that once she's calmed down.'

'Pregnancy makes you very emotional,' the other woman sympathized. 'Remember how sensitive we both were?'

Mattie shifted slightly sideways, twitching aside the curtain that separated her from the next booth. The two beautiful women who sat there were so alike that it didn't take two guesses for her to realize they had to be the Beauchamp twins, Sally and Cally.

Not only did they look alike, they bore a striking resemblance to their older brother Jack, both dark-haired and dark-eyed.

'I wonder what this girlfriend of Jack's is like?' mused the twin sitting on the left. 'I think we're all more excited about meeting her this evening than we are Sandy's engagement or Tina's pregnancy!'

Mattie quickly let the curtain drop back into place, her cheeks colouring a heated red at this enforced eavesdropping. But the manicurist hadn't quite finished painting the nails on her second hand, meaning she couldn't just get up and leave!

'Mum says she's absolutely charming,' the other twin

confided. 'Certainly nothing at all like the gold-digger we were all expecting Jack to end up with.'

Gold-digger?

'Jack can be such a softie,' his sister opined.

A softie? Jack? That didn't sound like the Jack that Mattie had come to know. And love!

'Mum insists she's nothing like that,' the other woman insisted lightly. 'But I'm sure whoever Jack decided to marry, that Mum would think she was charming. We all would. As long as it was Jack's choice.'

Mattie had heard enough!

Not that she could exactly blame Jack's twin sisters for their gossipy speculation concerning the female Jack had brought with him this weekend; they were bound to feel a certain amount of curiosity. She just hadn't liked the idea that they might imagine she was with Jack because of his money. It certainly put a completely different slant on how she was to behave this evening in front of Jack's family.

'Thank you,' she told the manicurist stiltedly, snatching her barely finished hand away to stand up. 'If I could just pay my bill...?'

No doubt these treatments were going to cost her an arm and a leg, but after the remarks she had just overheard there was no way Mattie was going to put it on Jack's hotel bill. Even if she had to live on bread and water for the next month!

The Beauchamp twins, enjoying their own manicure, glanced at Mattie as she moved stiffly across the salon after paying her bill. But as they could have no idea she was 'the girlfriend' they had so recently referred to, it was only a cursory glance.

Mattie wished she had followed her first instinct this

morning and left Paris before she'd had to meet any more of the Beauchamp family!

They were certainly an attractive lot. In fact, Mattie felt like the equivalent of the ugly duckling amongst such beautiful swans.

And Jack, no matter what his reasons were with regard to the sister of his future brother-in-law, had been utterly stupid to bring her here to meet them all!

They were all obviously expecting to hear wedding bells, assumed her presence here at all was some sort of declaration of intent on Jack's part.

Why hadn't Jack thought of that?

She shook her head impatiently, walking out of the hotel again instead of going back up to the suite she and Jack shared, torn now between a desire to pay Jack back for his deception in getting her to come to Paris with him in the first place, and a wish not to let him down in front of his obviously concerned, and loving, family.

As she sat on the grass near the Eiffel Tower Mattie knew that the latter easily won...

She wasn't naturally a vindictive person, and, from the little she had seen of them, the rest of Jack's family were as nice, and concerned for him, as his mother had been this morning.

So what did she do now?

Mattie had absolutely no idea!

She had left Jack to a mood of confusion earlier, had intended to continue to confuse him by her unexpected friendliness after the strain under which they had parted the evening before. But the reality of his family now made that an impossibility.

What a mess!

Of someone else's making for a change—namely,

Jack's! But, the woman Sharon apart, Mattie cared about Jack too much to let him down in front of his family this evening. Even if it galled her to have to continue to play the role of loving girlfriend!

'You look absolutely beautiful,' Jack told her with admiration as she joined him in the sitting-room shortly after seven o'clock that evening.

Mattie was wearing the second new evening dress she had bought for this weekend: a short-sleeved knee-length cream lace affair that brought out the honey tints in her newly washed and styled blonde hair.

'Thank you,' she accepted soberly.

This was the first time she had seen Jack since her return to the hotel, Jack seeming to have taken her advice and gone back to bed this afternoon. At least, the silence of the hotel suite had seemed to imply as much.

He certainly no longer looked haggard, at any rate!

In fact, once again wearing the black dinner suit and a white shirt, he looked altogether too lethally attractive for Mattie's peace of mind.

'Mattie, before we go I think I ought to—'

'Your mother rang through to the suite earlier,' Mattie effectively cut through on what Jack intended saying, avoiding looking at him as best she could; he was just altogether too much for her peace of mind. 'As you were asleep at the time, I took the call,' she explained as he raised surprised brows; although she had no idea what his parents must think of the two of them sharing a suite in this way! 'Apparently, we're all meeting in the bar downstairs at seven-fifteen for a drink before strolling over to the restaurant.'

Jack's frown deepened. 'We are?'

'We are,' Mattie confirmed briskly, moving pointedly towards the door. 'As it's almost that now, I suggest we go down...' She surveyed him with narrowed eyes as Jack looked less than eager to comply.

He gave a wince. 'Mattie, I was hoping for a chance to talk to you when we returned to the hotel last night—'

'But we were rudely interrupted,' she interjected.

'Yes,' he acknowledged grimly. 'There's something I really should tell you before we go downstairs to meet the family—'

'Tell me on the way,' she suggested, moving out into the carpeted corridor. Besides, she already knew what he really should tell her!

A little late in the day for confession time, she would have thought. Besides, she really didn't intend giving him the chance to confess anything; she might be under an obligation to Betty and the rest of the Beauchamp family to be on her best behaviour, but as far as Jack was concerned she felt no such compunction.

She wanted the satisfaction of seeing the shocked surprise on his face when she met his sisters and showed no surprise at their identity at all. She felt, after the way Jack had made her feel so guilty over her mix-up with the flowers, that she was owed that, at least.

Jack joined her out in the corridor, taking a firm grasp of her elbow as he prevented her from walking too fast. 'You see, Mattie,' he began with audible reluctance. 'I haven't—'

'Jack! Mattie! Wait for us!'

Mattie almost burst out laughing at the impatient frustration on Jack's face as they both recognized his mother's voice behind them. Poor Jack, he wasn't going to get the chance to make his confession, after all. She could almost feel sorry for him. As sorry as he'd made her over the mix-up with the flowers!

She turned to smile at Betty, her eyes widening slightly as she took in the man who walked at Betty's side; he was so like Jack, give or take another forty years, that this had to be Edward Beauchamp. Mattie felt she would have been able to recognize exactly who he was—Betty's husband—anyway.

Tall, much taller than his wife, dark hair threaded through with grey, his face an older version of Jack's good looks. They really *were* a very attractive family, Mattie decided.

'Mattie, this is my husband Edward,' Betty introduced warmly, looking extremely regal in a long black sequinned gown. 'Edward, this is Jack's friend, Mattie.'

Even the eyes were the same warm brown, Mattie discovered as she looked up into the aristocratically handsome face of Edward Beauchamp as the two of them shook hands.

'It's a pleasure to meet you,' Edward told her with sincerity.

'Isn't this nice?' Betty proclaimed happily as she linked arms with Mattie with the friendliness that seemed to be such a part of her nature, the two women walking ahead of the men now as they made their way to the lift. 'The girls are all absolutely furious that I've stolen a march on them and met you first,' she confided conspiratorially, obviously immensely pleased with herself for having done so, too.

Mattie was glad that Jack wasn't in hearing distance of that last remark. Just a few minutes fun, that was all she wanted. Just to see Jack squirm for a little bit, as he had made her squirm.

Was that being vindictive, after all? she wondered. No, she concluded; it was only for a few minutes, and after that, no matter how she might personally feel about practising such a deception on this charming family, she would do her best to help Jack get through what promised to be a very uncomfortable evening for him.

Even if it was of his own making!

CHAPTER NINE

'COULD I just borrow Mattie for a few minutes?' Jack asked as the four of them approached the hotel bar, the sound of people chattering audible over the soft playing of a piano.

Mattie turned to look at him, her arm still linked with Betty's. Jack had the look of a man about to face the executioner!

She moved away from Betty to now link her arm with Jack's, looking up at him unconcernedly. 'I'm sure there will be plenty of time for us to talk later, Jack,' she assured him brightly; she could easily feel the tension in his arm beneath her fingertips.

He looked less than reassured. 'But—'

'The girls are going to be so disappointed if I tell them you've been delayed,' his mother warned him with light reproval.

Almost as if Betty knew what Mattie was doing. Although Jack's mother couldn't possibly know. Could she...?

'Come on, son.' His father gave him a playful slap on the back. 'You know what the Beauchamp women are like. Besides, it will be less—momentous, for Mattie, if the four of us go in together.'

Well, at least one member of this family appreciated how difficult Mattie was finding this meeting with them! Even if Edward couldn't fully appreciate why!

'Let's go in, Jack,' she encouraged. 'It will be all

right,' she relented enough to reassure him as she saw how truly miserable he was looking.

But it was of his own making, she reasoned to herself as he reluctantly complied. Why hadn't he just told her the truth in the first place? It would have been so much simpler.

The sisters were all there in the bar. Sandy laughing softly with a tall dark-haired man, the love shining out of her face proclaiming him as Thom, her new fiancé, Tina was talking with a slightly stocky man who was probably the insensitive Jim; Sally was with a tall blond-haired man, and Cally's choice of husband was a tall red-haired man Mattie thought might be a Scot. There was also another older couple present, who were probably the new fiancé's parents. However, there was no sign yet of their daughter, Sharon.

As the four of them approached all conversation ceased between the other members of the Beauchamp family as they turned to look, and Mattie could feel Jack's tension deepen as he reached down to tightly clasp her hand in his.

He really was worried about this meeting!

What did he think she was going to do, for goodness' sake? Even if she hadn't been aware of exactly who Tina, Sandy, Cally, and Sally were, she believed she could be trusted not to make a scene in front of Jack's family!

Although Jack obviously wasn't as sure!

Mattie relented slightly in the face of Jack's increasing misery, standing on tiptoe to whisper softly in his ear. 'Just introduce me, Jack; it's going to be fine.'

He swallowed hard. 'I just wish you had let me explain—'

'Do it later.' She gave an encouraging squeeze of his hand. 'And please don't worry—'

'Hi, everyone!' greeted a huskily sexy voice from close behind them. 'I do hope I'm not too late?' the woman added insincerely.

Jack had stiffened at Mattie's side at the first sound of that come-to-bed voice. Mattie gave him a concerned look before turning slowly to look at the newcomer.

The woman was tall, with flowing dark hair that reached down to her waist. The short, figure-hugging tube-dress she was wearing was the same deep violet colour as her eyes—eyes framed by the longest dark lashes Mattie had ever seen, her face having the delicate beauty of an exquisite china doll.

This was Thom's sister, Sharon?

She had to be. Everyone else in the family was already present.

This was the woman Jack claimed he needed protecting from?

Mattie glanced at him consideringly. If that was how Jack really felt, then he must be the only man in the room who did!

Because every other man present, whether alone or with someone, was unashamedly staring at the beautiful woman who was now laughingly greeting Sandy and Thom, before moving on to the other sisters and their respective spouses.

But even as the woman chatted and laughed with the rest of the family, Mattie was conscious of the fact that Sharon was completely aware of Jack as he stood stiffly at Mattie's side, could sense the other woman's interest even before she finally came to stand directly in front of him.

'Jack,' Sharon initiated.

He gave a polite inclination of his head. 'Sharon.'

'I'm sure we can do better than that; after all, we'll soon be one big, happy family!' Sharon murmured throatily before leaning forward and kissing him lightly on the lips, effectively prompting the release of Jack's hand from Mattie's as he reached up to clasp the slenderness of Sharon's tanned, bared shoulders and moved her firmly away from him. 'It's so good to see you again,' Sharon persisted, now determinedly linking her arm with his in forced intimacy.

Mattie had heard other women use the phrase, 'I just want to scratch her eyes out', although she had never before felt such an inclination herself. But at that moment she knew she could cheerfully have carried out such a threat on the beautiful Sharon!

How dared Sharon look at Jack in that way, as if she just wanted to devour him? As if, for her, no one else in the room existed?

Although, to give Jack his due, he wasn't giving the woman any encouragement—

He didn't need to!

Sharon looked like a woman who knew what she wanted. And got it, too. And she obviously wanted Jack Beauchamp.

What Mattie didn't understand was why Jack didn't want Sharon in return. Or, at least, said he didn't...

But why should he lie about such a thing? It didn't—

'—me introduce you to my friend, Mattie Crawford,' Jack was saying now, his arm moving lightly about Mattie's waist as he pulled her to his side. 'Mattie, this is Sharon Keswick, Thom's sister.'

'And I thought we were so much more than that,

Jack,' the other woman taunted before turning hard violet-coloured eyes on Mattie. 'It's nice to meet you,
Mandy,' she greeted disinterestedly, her handshake definitely on the limp side too.

'Mattie,' she corrected, releasing her hand as quickly
as possible, having no doubts that the use of the wrong
name had been deliberate on the other woman's part, at
the same time deciding there was absolutely no point in
returning any nicety of her own; she wouldn't mean it
any more than the other woman did.

'Mattie,' Sharon corrected in a bored voice, the light
of challenge in those violet-coloured eyes now. 'Have
we met before? Perhaps you know the—'

'Can I get you some champagne, Sharon?' Edward
Beauchamp stepped in to offer politely.

'If you'll both excuse us?' Jack cut in dismissively. 'I
just want to introduce Mattie to the rest of the family.'

Considering that a few minutes ago it was the last
thing he had wanted to do…!

'What a good idea,' Mattie agreed. 'I'm sure we'll
talk again later in the evening, Miss Keswick,' she told
the other woman coolly.

'You can count on it,' Sharon murmured before turning smilingly to Edward Beauchamp and accepting the
glass of champagne he held out to her.

'Whew!' Jack breathed deeply once they were safely
out of earshot. 'See what I mean?' he added grimly.

Mattie wasn't at all sure what she was supposed to
see. Sharon *was* as interested in Jack as he had claimed
she was—more than interested!—and he was as obviously fighting shy of that interest.

But surely there had been more to the encounter than

that, an underlying something, a feeling that some sort of intimacy did exist between the two of them?

One thing Mattie did know: all the fun had gone out of the evening for her. She had intended teasing Jack a little concerning the identity of his four sisters, of having just a little fun at his expense, but now she felt no such inclination. In fact, as far as Mattie was concerned, with Sharon Keswick's arrival she stopped enjoying herself!

Mainly because, as Sharon hadn't been present when they'd arrived downstairs, a part of Mattie had begun to wonder if there really was a Sharon at all, if it hadn't just been another part of the game Jack was playing with her. Because if that were the case, then there was the possibility that perhaps Jack had invited her to Paris with him for an altogether different reason...

But all those half-hopes and dreams had disappeared out of the window the moment the other woman had put in an appearance. And what an appearance!

Mattie once again felt like that ugly duckling amongst so many beautiful swans. One beautiful swan in particular...!

'All I saw was a beautiful woman,' Mattie snapped abruptly.

'Oh, she's certainly that,' Jack conceded ruefully.

Mattie bridled resentfully; he could have at least attempted to play down the other woman's beauty—even if it weren't the truth! 'Then where's your problem?' she returned scathingly.

Jack gave a shake of his head. 'It's too complicated to explain right now—'

'I'm sure that if you use simple words, ones with only two syllables or less, that I'll understand!' Mattie scorned.

Jack turned to her looking worried. 'Mattie—'

'Not now, Jack,' she interrupted, forcing herself to smile as they approached his family group. 'Now you have to introduce me to your four sisters: Tina, the twins Sally and Cally, and Sandy,' she recited.

Even the stunned look on Jack's face as he came to an abrupt halt at this announcement didn't give her the satisfaction she had expected it would. Because the arrival of the beautiful Sharon Keswick had completely taken the shine off the evening as far as Mattie was concerned.

'If I were you, Jack, I would stop my impersonation of a goldfish, and introduce me,' she told him, still smiling—even if she felt more like crying. 'Your sisters and their partners are all wondering what's keeping us.' In fact, the younger members of his family were all discreetly looking the other way as she and Jack talked softly together. No doubt they were under the impression that she and Jack were murmuring sweet intimacies to each other.

No such luck!

This would teach her to believe there might be such a thing as happy-ever-after for her with Jack. Jack himself had claimed from the beginning that he wanted her with him in Paris as a deterrent to the attentions of Sharon Keswick, and the last few minutes had shown her that was the truth. Nothing less. But certainly nothing more.

She had envisaged that this evening, she would finally forgive him for his little subterfuge, and then hopefully the two of them could spend the rest of the evening together enjoying themselves. They might even have ended the evening in the way that they could have done last night if his sister hadn't interrupted them…

None of that was going to happen now!

It was her own fault, of course. Jack had been pleasant to her, a wonderful companion the evening before, but he had never given any indication that he felt more than that. She was the one who had made the mistake of falling in love with him.

'You know!' he finally stopped his impersonation of a goldfish—his mouth opening and closing but no sound coming out—long enough to gasp incredulously.

'Of course I know,' she said snippily. 'Ha ha, very funny.' She grimaced. 'Satisfied?'

Jack still looked completely stunned. 'But I— How—? When—?'

'Your mother. This morning,' she answered the unfinished questions. 'Does this happen very often?' she teased, realizing there was really no point in the two of them falling out; the beautiful Sharon Keswick or not, they still had this evening to get through with the rest of Jack's family.

He blinked. 'What?'

'A speechless Jack Beauchamp!' she replied with satisfaction.

His gaze narrowed. 'You've known the truth since this morning…?'

'The early bird catches the gossip,' she misquoted.

'Hmm,' Jack mused suspiciously. 'My mother didn't mention any of this when I spoke to her earlier this afternoon.'

He must have gone to see his mother after Mattie had disappeared to the beauty salon…

'Well, she wouldn't have done, would she?' Mattie retorted, slipping her arm into the crook of his. 'Your poor mother had no idea I ever believed Tina, Sally, Cally, and Sandy were anything other than your four younger sisters!' She gave him an overbright smile.

'Of course not,' Jack conceded slowly, his gaze narrowed on the insincerity of her smile. 'So that was the reason for your unexpected—friendliness, earlier when I returned from the airport; you were playing with me, Mattie Crawford,' he realized ruefully.

'At your own game, Jack Beauchamp,' she acknowledged dryly, thankfully latching onto this explanation; she had been playing with him earlier, but her feelings for him were very real. And she didn't want him to even guess at those!

'Touché.' He gave an inclination of his head, his eyes gleaming with laughter as he draped his arm casually about her shoulders. 'In that case, let's go and say hello to the clan!'

'The clan', as he called them, were only too pleased to meet her, all his sisters warm and friendly, the men teasingly congratulating Jack on catching himself such a lovely girlfriend.

Mattie was grateful for the warmth of their compliments, needed all the ego-boosting there was going after that confrontation with Sharon Keswick.

In contrast, Sharon's brother, Thom, was charming and friendly, with none of that brittle hardness that was such a part of his beautiful sister's nature.

'Has Mattie realized yet that you're a workaholic, Jack?' Thom teased his future brother-in-law.

Jack's arm tightened about Mattie's shoulders.

'Maybe that will change now that I have Mattie,' he answered suggestively.

'Or that you're a lousy golf player?' Ian, Cally's Scottish husband, joked. 'He has a handicap of twenty-four,' he confided in Mattie disgustedly.

'I'm better suited to indoor sports,' Jack returned smoothly.

'In that case, has Mattie realized yet that you snore—? Ouch!' Jim gave an aggrieved look in the direction of his wife, at the same time rubbing the ankle Tina had just kicked.

Mattie had been smiling from the beginning of this teasing of Jack, but now she couldn't help bursting out laughing; poor Jim, he really did have a way of putting his foot in his mouth!

'I really am sorry for the way I barged into your evening last night,' Tina told her self-consciously. 'I don't know what you must have thought of me. And I kept poor Jack awake for hours with my emotional ranting and raving,' she confessed.

No wonder he had looked so tired when he'd returned from the airport earlier...

'Don't give it another thought.' Mattie squeezed the other woman's arm understandingly. 'That's what families are for. Besides, it's all settled now. And I understand congratulations are in order...?' She looked at the newly expectant parents.

'Thank you,' Tina accepted glowingly. 'And just ignore this idiot of a husband of mine,' she added, at the same time moving closer to Jim to smile at him lovingly. 'His brain very often doesn't connect with his mouth!'

'So that's what his problem is,' Jack mused affectionately. 'And I thought he was just socially inept.'

'That too,' Tina agreed.

'When the two of you have quite finished discussing my shortcomings…!' Jim protested.

'We haven't even started yet!' Jack warned him.

'Time we were all making a move, I think,' Betty put in softly, she and Edward having spent the last few minutes chatting with Thom's parents.

The Keswicks looked like nice, ordinary people too, both short and slightly plump, making Mattie wonder how on earth they could have produced a daughter like Sharon…and not just her beautiful looks!

'Just what else did you and my mother talk about when you met this morning?' Jack enquired as they all strolled over to the Eiffel Tower. 'Besides inadvertently telling you exactly who Tina, Sally, Cally, and Sandy are, she obviously told you about Tina's pregnancy too.'

Mattie raised innocent brows. 'I find your mother very easy to talk to.'

'Unlike me.' He grimaced.

Oh, she found Jack easy to talk to too. Too easy. Which was why she had to be constantly on her guard not to reveal exactly how she felt about him.

Mattie hesitated. 'I—'

'It really is so good to see you again, Jack,' Sharon Keswick drawled suggestively as she strolled over to walk on his other side, unhesitatingly linking her arm with his. 'I do hope you'll excuse us, *Mandy*.' She leant around Jack to show perfect white teeth in another of those insincere smiles. 'But Jack and I are old friends,' she explained, looking up at Jack beneath those incredible lashes now. 'Isn't this just the most romantic place on earth, Jack?' she exclaimed breathlessly, those violet eyes wide and beguiling as she gazed up at the star-lit sky.

Mattie—Mandy?—couldn't help wondering just how 'old' the friendship between Jack and Sharon was…?

She also distinctly disliked the way the other woman kept touching Jack with every opportunity she had, as if she had a perfect right to do so. Which was ridiculous; it was really none of Mattie's business who touched Jack. Or, more importantly, who Jack allowed to touch him. Because, despite his earlier comments, he wasn't exactly fighting the other woman off *now*, was he?

Which was why Mattie wasn't exactly surprised when Sharon managed to manoeuvre herself into the seat on the other side of Jack at the huge round table they were all seated at for dinner.

She wasn't surprised—but she was furious. With Jack. With Sharon Keswick. But most of all with herself—for having been so foolish as to fall in love with a man who was so out of her reach!

CHAPTER TEN

'I REALLY wouldn't worry too much about my little sister, if I were you,' Thom, seated on Mattie's other side, reassured her some time later.

Mattie turned to give him a strained smile, her head pounding, her appetite for the first course they had already been served almost nil, her appreciation for the illuminated romantic Paris skyline even less. And all because of, as Thom had guessed so rightly, his sister Sharon.

Despite Jack's attempts to include Mattie in the conversation, the other woman had completely dominated Jack's attention since they'd sat down. If Mattie heard Sharon begin one more sentence with, 'Do you remember, Jack, when we', she truly believed she was going to scream!

Just what sort of old friends were Jack and Sharon?

Not that it took two guesses to find the answer to that! Which made Jack's reasons for dragging Mattie all the way here all the more—

'He isn't interested, you know,' Thom spoke again, softly.

Mattie's smile was scathing this time; Jack had certainly been interested at some time in the not-so-distant past!

'He really isn't, Mattie,' Thom insisted, his hand resting briefly on hers as she shredded the bread roll on her side plate into inedible pieces.

Mattie glanced down impatiently at the mess that had once been the roll, rubbing the crumbs from her fingers back onto the plate. 'I would hate to see what he looks like when he is interested, then,' she said disgustedly, at the same time shooting Jack's partially turned shoulders an irritated glance as Sharon continued to monopolise him.

Thom laughed. 'Try looking at him when he's with you,' he suggested gently. 'I've certainly never seen Jack looking as relaxed and happy as he was with you when we were all chatting together earlier.'

Mattie frowned her puzzlement at this comment. 'But I've only ever seen Jack relaxed and happy,' she said slowly.

'Exactly,' his future brother-in-law said.

Mattie really had no idea what Thom was talking about. Jack was a man completely sure of himself, of who he was, and where he was going. But, then, Thom also didn't know that her being here with Jack at all was just an act on his part...

Which just went to prove what a good actor he was!

For all the good it had done; Jack had spent most of the evening talking to Sharon Keswick, anyway. Mattie's presence here really was superfluous.

She gave a shake of her head. 'I appreciate your concern, Thom, but it really isn't necessary.' Her smile made her face ache. 'Jack and I don't have that sort of relationship.' They didn't have a relationship at all! After this weekend she very much doubted she would ever see him again.

Thom shrugged. 'Then perhaps you should.'

Mattie's eyes widened. Not that she was a prude or anything, but it sounded rather odd having Jack's future brother-in-law advising her to advance her relationship with Jack onto a physical one.

Not that she hadn't thought about it, but—

'I wouldn't want you to make the same mistake I did with Sandy five years ago, Mattie,' Thom continued candidly. 'We dated for a while then,' he explained at Mattie's questioning look. 'I knew I loved her, that she was the only woman I could ever marry—I just forgot to tell her that! Needless to say, someone else came along and told her all the things she needed to hear. Before I knew what had happened, she was married to that someone else.' He sighed. 'I had to wait another four years for her to decide she had made a mistake, for her to be free so that I could finally tell her how I felt about her.'

That was hardly the case with Mattie and Jack, was it? She might be in love with Jack, but he certainly didn't feel that way about her, would probably run a mile in the opposite direction if she were to tell him she was in love with him—

'What are you two talking about so seriously?' Jack broke into her troubled thoughts.

Although the hard glitter in those dark brown eyes in no way reflected the friendliness of his tone! In fact, he looked distinctly angry. Because she was talking to Thom? Well, that was ridiculous when he had spent the majority of the evening so far talking to Sharon!

'I—'

'I was just telling Mattie—' Thom spoke decisively

over what was going to be Mattie's sharp reply '—that I lost your sister five years ago because I was too stupid to tell her how I felt about her.' He looked challengingly at Jack.

Mattie felt embarrassed colour enter her cheeks; Jack was going to wonder how on earth she and Thom could have got onto such a personal subject in the space of a few minutes!

Jack steadily returned Thom's gaze for several long seconds. 'Really?' he finally drawled.

'Yes—really,' the other man echoed firmly.

For goodness' sake, this was supposed to be a family celebration—and Jack and Thom were eyeing each other as if they were sizing each other up for a fight!

'And I was just saying how romantic it all was that they have finally got together,' Mattie put in brightly.

'Women are very big on romance, Jack,' Thom pronounced. 'You should try it some time,' he added dryly.

Jack's expression darkened. 'With a family like mine that can sometimes be rather difficult,' he returned tightly.

Enigmatically, as far as Mattie was concerned. All she did know was that she had to break up this conversation—challenge? After all, they were here to celebrate Thom and Sandy's engagement.

But Sandy joined in the conversation before she could say anything else. 'After the complete mess you made of sending our Easter flowers, Jack, you're lucky any of the female members of this family is actually speaking to you,' she admonished her older brother. 'Luckily we all have a sense of humour! It was really rather funny, Mattie,' she turned to confide. 'Jack sent us all flowers, but with all the wrong cards attached. Think of the fun it would have been if we had all been his girlfriends instead of his sisters!'

Jack looked nonplussed. 'Yes—just think.' He gave a challenging glance in Mattie's direction.

Mattie, who just wanted to crawl under the table and hide!

She was also aware that Thom was studying her closely, that he could no doubt see the embarrassed expression on her face, the warning glare she had just shot in Jack's direction.

'It's just as well you're a one-woman man, isn't it, Jack?' Thom murmured slowly.

'Isn't it?' Jack returned noncommittally, his gaze still holding Mattie's.

'Whereas we all thought it was a scream.' Sandy chuckled.

'It does sound rather—amusing,' Mattie acknowledged hollowly.

'That depends how you look at it,' Jack derided.

'He didn't muddle the card up on your flowers too, did he, Mattie?' Sandy continued mischievously. 'You really would have thought it strange if you had received flowers with a card on to Tina, Sally, Cally, or Sandy!'

Mattie gave a weak smile, knowing it was best not to mention that she hadn't received any flowers at all—just blackmail threats!

'I think we should stop teasing poor Jack,' Thom cut in. 'You haven't told us what you do for a living, Mattie?' he asked interestedly, blue eyes gently probing as he looked at her.

'What makes you think she does anything?' Sharon,

obviously deciding she had been excluded from the conversation quite long enough, put in scathingly. 'After all, Jack is a very wealthy man, aren't you, darling?' She once again looked at him beneath those long, dark lashes.

Thom shot his sister a dismissive glance. 'Because most women prefer to work nowadays, Sharon,' he told her patiently.

'I don't,' she dismissed in a bored voice.

'I said most women, Sharon,' her brother derided before turning back to look questioningly at Mattie.

Mattie knew that if she told them she was a florist then the game would most definitely be up; she already knew that all the members of this family were intelligent enough to add two and two together and come up with the appropriate answer of four!

'I'm a contracts manager,' she supplied noncommittally. 'And in my spare time,' she added—before anyone could ask any more questions!— 'I help my mother run a boarding-kennels.'

'Speaking of which... How's Harry doing, Jack?' Sandy prompted concernedly.

Obviously, from the warmth of Sandy's voice as she talked of Harry, the Bearded Collie was a favourite with all the Beauchamp family. Mattie was glad, having decided long ago that anyone who liked dogs and children was okay with her. And she couldn't help liking the Beauchamp family. More than liking one of them!

'Ask Mattie.' Jack smiled. 'Harry is staying at her mother's kennels,' he explained at Thom and Sandy's questioning looks.

'That makes sense,' Sandy agreed. 'Has he settled

down okay, Mattie? Jack has been so worried about boarding him, he almost didn't come to Paris at all!'

Mattie couldn't quite believe that was true; Jack's was obviously a very close family.

Even those members of it who really weren't any sort of relation at all, she thought with a glance in Sharon Keswick's direction.

'You were the one who spoke to my mother yesterday, Jack,' Mattie reminded him with a lingering resentment; she would have liked to speak to her mother yesterday too, but Jack hadn't even given her the option!

'Harry has himself a girlfriend,' Jack revealed with a grin. 'A rather beautiful Labrador named Sophie,' he explained affectionately.

'There seems to be a lot of it about,' Thom murmured tongue-in-cheek. 'You know, Jack—' He broke off as the waiters started to arrive with their main courses.

The next few minutes were taken up by the arrival of the food, and the admiring remarks on its presentation and wonderful smells, by which time the subject of what Mattie did for a living had been well and truly dropped.

Much to her relief!

Thom, much as she found his company pleasant, didn't seem to be as convinced as the rest of the family by the relationship between Jack and herself. Despite his earlier comments, he seemed to have realized there was more to the relationship than either of them were telling. Or less, as actually was the case!

'Good?' Jack prompted after Mattie had tasted her first mouthful of the mouth-watering chicken she had ordered for her main course.

'Very,' she confirmed abruptly.

Jack sighed. 'Mattie, other than being downright rude to the woman, what can I do about the situation?'

Her eyes widened at his defensive attitude. 'Did I say anything?'

'You didn't need to,' he muttered. 'I could feel your disapproval burning into my shoulder blades!'

Had her feelings earlier been that obvious? To Thom, obviously. But to Jack, too? That would never do!

She forced a smile to her lips, aware that Betty Beauchamp, sitting across the other side of the huge table, was watching them with an indulgent smile on her lips. 'I was merely wondering why you bothered to bring me with you at all when you so obviously enjoy Sharon's company,' she said with saccharine sweetness.

'Enjoy her company...!' Jack's expression darkened. 'I would like to wring her damned neck!'

Mattie couldn't help it; she laughed. Jack looked so much like a disgruntled little boy, it was difficult not to.

'That's better.' Jack's expression brightened, before he leant forward to kiss her softly on the mouth. 'Seeing you laugh is like watching the sun come out,' he explained at her stunned expression.

'Oh,' she accepted shyly, feeling suddenly self-conscious with all of his family sitting around them.

But, then, that was the point, wasn't it? she instantly reasoned with herself. She mustn't take that kiss too seriously; Jack was merely putting on an act for his family. And Sharon Keswick.

Because the other woman, as Mattie glanced over Jack's shoulder, looked absolutely furious at this public display of affection between Jack and Mattie. In fact, if looks could kill...!

'Well, that seems to have worked,' Mattie told Jack wryly. 'Sharon isn't at all happy about that kiss.'

He shook his head. 'Mattie, that isn't the reason I—'

'Smile, Jack,' Mattie told him softly. 'Your mother is watching us, too.'

He frowned darkly. 'I don't give a damn—'

'Well, I do,' Mattie cut in firmly. 'I happen to like your mother very much.'

Jack gave her a considering look, a sudden grin lighting his features even as he reached out and squeezed Mattie's hand. 'From what she said to me a few minutes ago, I think she likes you too,' he confided gruffly.

Mattie would have liked to know what it was his mother had said to him, but at that moment Edward Beauchamp stood up to make a short speech to toast his daughter and her fiancé, finishing his speech by adding that he hoped they would all be together again like this for the wedding in three months' time.

Three months' time...

What would Mattie be doing in three months' time? Not seeing Jack, that was for sure.

Which thought was enough, once again, to rob her of her appetite. At this rate, she would have lost weight by the time she left Paris!

'As today was such a disaster, is there anything you would especially like to do tomorrow?' Jack had no such qualms, eating his steak with enthusiasm as he waited for her answer.

'We all thought of going to Notre-Dame tomorrow,' Sandy was the one to answer him. 'Making a family outing of it. Do you remember the family picnics, Jack?' she reminded him wistfully.

'Ants in the sandwiches and flies in the ice creams.' He nodded.

'Trust you to remember that part of it!' Sandy laughed.

Mattie could only sit and listen in fascination as Jack and Sandy started to reminisce about some of their more hilarious family holidays. As an only child, on her own with her mother from the age of three, this shared sibling fun was all new to her.

One thing she did become very aware of as the rest of the evening passed in pleasantly uncomplicated conversation—somehow Jack managed to continue to exclude Sharon Keswick from most of it!—was that to be accepted into the warmth exuded by the Beauchamp family was like being taken into a charmed circle.

It became more and more difficult for Mattie, as the evening progressed, for her to realize that as far as she was concerned she was only a part of this for a few days, that on her return to England on Monday she would probably never see Jack again…

'Mattie and I are going for a stroll,' Jack announced determinedly as they all left the Eiffel Tower several hours later.

'A stroll, hmm, Jack?' As usual Jim said exactly what he thought.

'Whatever.' Jack shrugged, grinning at the other man, his arm about Mattie's shoulders.

'I think I'll join you,' Sharon Keswick had once again managed to manoeuvre herself on Jack's other side. 'I could do with some fresh air after being cooped up for hours.'

Considering there had been a cool air-flow in the restaurant, as well as the room being brightly lit and airy, Mattie found this excuse rather lame. But at least Jack didn't look too thrilled by the prospect of being joined by the other woman, either.

Her own heart had given an emotional leap at Jack's suggestion, only to plunge down into the depths of despair at the thought of once again sharing him with the pushy Sharon.

'Why don't we all go?' suggested one of the twins.

Cally, Mattie thought, although it was a little difficult to tell the two women apart this evening; both were wearing black dresses, their shoulder-length hair styled the same. Whichever one, Mattie was grateful for her intervention; she could imagine nothing more excruciating than strolling in the moonlight with Jack and Sharon Keswick!

'What a wonderful idea,' Betty Beauchamp took up the conversation. 'It's years since we've strolled together in the moonlight in Paris, isn't it, Edward?' She looked up adoringly at her husband.

'I believe Jack was the result of our last stroll here,' Edward returned dryly.

'Well, at least we know that isn't going to happen to us again,' Betty teased. To the amusement of the rest of the family.

'No, but with the obvious exclusion of Tina, it could happen to one of the others,' her husband reasoned ruefully.

'I already have a boy and a girl, so I've done my bit,' one of the twins protested.

'And we've decided to stop at one,' the other twin assured everyone.

'Well, don't look at us,' Jack advised, his arm tightening about Mattie's shoulders. 'Much as I love my niece and nephews, I want Mattie to myself for a while before we think about having children.'

'Let's all just take a stroll and see what happens, hmm?' His mother laughed affectionately, her arm linked again with her husband's.

Mattie was only too happy to begin their walk, her cheeks fiery red after that last conversation. Obviously close families had their drawbacks as well as their pluses!

'Before we have children'?' she queried as Jack strode a little ahead of the rest of the family, their close proximity meaning he swept Mattie along with him.

Jack scowled. 'Well, I had to say something, didn't I?' he bit out.

Mattie gave him a considering look. 'They were all only joking, Jack,' she chided.

Surely, if anyone should have been disconcerted by that particular conversation, it should have been her, and, embarrassing as it had been, it really had only been in fun.

'I know that.' Jack sighed heavily, glancing back impatiently at the rest of his family as they strolled happily along behind them. 'It's just—it's a conspiracy, that's what it is!'

'What is?' Mattie prompted.

'Last night and today taken up with Tina and Jim's problems, and now this evening the rest of the family seem determined not to give us any time alone together.' He shook his head impatiently. 'It's a family conspiracy!'

Mattie looked at his disgruntled expression, his whole demeanour one of tense irritation. He looked as if he would like to strangle someone. Anyone!

She bit her lips as they began to twitch with amusement, desperately trying not to laugh. And losing.

'And just what is so funny?' Jack turned to look at her in amazement as the chuckle she had been trying to hold in burst out anyway.

'You are,' she told him once she had sobered slightly. 'I'm sure that not one member of your family has any deliberate intention of intruding. Besides—' her humour faded completely now '—have you completely forgotten that this is all only an act, anyway?'

Jack looked down at her. '"Completely" forgotten…?'

Mattie pulled a face. 'Well, Sharon Keswick wasn't in the least put off by our supposed relationship, was she?'

'Are you implying that's my fault?' he said softly.

'Well, it certainly isn't mine,' Mattie defended protestingly.

Jack drew in a ragged breath, before releasing that same breath in a deep sigh. 'No,' he accepted heavily. 'The problem is, Mattie, that—several years ago, I made the mistake of going out with Sharon for a few weeks—'

'You didn't tell me that!' Not that she had needed telling after this evening; it had been all too obvious by the other woman's behaviour that she thought she had some sort of proprietorial claim on Jack.

'No one likes owning up to making a mistake.'

'I owned up to mine,' Mattie reminded him.

And look where it had got her! In Paris certainly,

which was wonderful. But falling in love with Jack, a man far beyond her reach, wasn't quite so wonderful…!

Jack gave a disgusted snort. 'Sharon looks—gorgeous—'

'I can see that,' Mattie snapped. She really didn't want to hear this!

'Well, looks aren't everything,' Jack told her irritably. 'The woman is a nightmare. I only went out with her three or four times—that's all, Mattie, I swear,' he insisted at her sceptical look. 'On the basis of those three or four dates, she tried to take over my life. Believe me, Mattie, there is nothing more off-putting to a man than a woman who tries to do that on the basis of a few weeks' acquaintance. I couldn't get away fast enough! Which is why it was very awkward when Sandy and Thom got together again a few months ago.'

Mattie could appreciate that. But could she also believe that Jack was immune to the other woman's obvious beauty…?

What did it matter what she believed? Another two days and none of this would be any of her business— it was none of her business now, for goodness' sake! And no matter how she felt about Jack, she had to keep remembering that!

'I'm sure it will all work out,' she assured Jack.

Jack glanced down at her. 'Sorry to bore you with my problems,' he apologised.

'I'm not bored,' Mattie instantly responded—as if she ever could be, in Jack's company! 'I'm just sorry I haven't been more of a help. If it's any consolation, I think a definite frost set in after the kiss,' she told him teasingly.

'The kiss…? Oh.' He nodded. 'Perhaps we should try it again?' he suggested, coming to a halt as they stood on the bridge that faced the Eiffel Tower, completely unconcerned by his family walking by as he turned Mattie towards him, his hands linked at the base of her spine.

Mattie looked up at him with wide blue eyes, her breath seeming to be lodged in her throat somewhere, very much aware of the way Jack's hips and thighs pressed against hers.

Jack's gaze held hers as he slowly bent his head, his mouth gently touching hers, her lips parting instinctively as the kiss deepened, her arms moving up about his shoulders as she clung to him.

The rest of the world ceased to exist as Mattie became lost in the wonder of that kiss, in the sheer physical force that was Jack, in the warm desire zinging through her body. At that moment, she felt, the Eiffel Tower itself could have toppled over, and neither of them would have been aware of it!

Jack was the one to finally break the kiss, to rest the warmth of his forehead on hers as he looked down at her flushed face with eyes darkened with desire.

Mattie trembled with that same desire, knowing that she wanted Jack. Desperately. Completely.

'Are you cold?' Jack asked as he misunderstood the reason for her trembling. 'Here.' He stepped back to slip off his dinner jacket and drape it about her shoulders. 'Let's go back to the hotel, hmm?' he offered gruffly.

'Yes,' Mattie agreed unhesitantly, the heat of desire coursing through her body making her feel that she would never be cold again, although the feel and smell of Jack's jacket about her shoulders was wonderful.

Their hands linked, their gazes locked, she was barely aware of the walk back to the hotel, certainly had no idea what had happened to the rest of the family; she just wanted to be alone with Jack, to fulfil the promise of the kiss they had just shared.

'Miss Crawford? Miss Crawford, there is a telephone message for you!' a pretty young girl at Reception called out to her as she and Jack walked past the desk.

Mattie blinked, the girl's words taking several seconds to penetrate the fog in her brain that had developed as she thought only of Jack and the time when they could be alone together.

'For me?' she finally repeated, looking up at Jack in bewilderment. 'But no one knows that I'm—my mother!' she suddenly realized with panic, that fog instantly clearing as her mind began to race with possible reasons why her mother should have telephoned her here.

'Calm down, Mattie,' Jack soothed, walking over to the desk with her. 'Diana probably just wants to know if you're having a good time. Thank you.' He smiled at the receptionist as he took the white envelope she held out to them. 'Let's take this up to our room and read it, hmm?' he encouraged as Mattie hurriedly took the envelope from him.

There was no way that Mattie could wait until then to open the envelope and read her message, ripping it open there and then, her eyes widening, her face paling, as she saw the message.

'What is it?' Jack demanded. 'Mattie, is it your mother—?'

'It's Harry,' she burst out emotionally, tears in her eyes as she looked up at Jack. 'My mother says that she had to call the vet in to him this morning, that he—that he's very ill. Oh, Jack!' she cried tearfully as she saw his face pale to a sickly grey colour.

CHAPTER ELEVEN

'HARRY'S going to be fine, Jack,' Mattie assured him late the following afternoon as the two of them drove away from Heathrow Airport. 'When I spoke to my mother again this morning she said Harry was slightly better,' she reminded him as he still looked grim.

They had put through a call to her mother the evening before as soon as they'd reached the hotel suite. Diana had waited up in expectation of their call, had explained calmly and clearly that Harry had developed a chest infection, but had been treated by a vet, and was even now asleep in his basket in their kitchen.

This had done little to reassure Jack as he'd paced the floor of their hotel suite all night. Mattie had ordered pot after pot of coffee from Room Service as she'd sat up with him, both of them impatient for the morning so that they could get booked onto a flight back to London.

Another telephone call to her mother before they'd left the hotel this morning had assured them that Harry was no worse, that in fact his condition seemed to be improving.

But Jack, Mattie knew, was still intensely worried, barely speaking on the flight back to England, his expression grim.

Mattie reached out and lightly touched his arm. 'You couldn't have known, Jack,' she consoled him gently, knowing that part of his problem was that he felt guilty about leaving Harry in the first place. 'None of us could,' she added; it would be just too awful if Jack blamed her mother for Harry becoming ill.

A conspiracy, Jack had called it the previous evening. And, after this last disaster, Mattie had to say that she agreed with him. Every time she and Jack seemed to become in the least close, something happened to part them again.

Because they *were* apart, Jack completely remote and uncommunicative, nothing Mattie said or did seeming to penetrate the wall he had built around himself since the previous evening and they'd learnt how sick Harry was.

Did Jack hold her mother responsible? If he did, then he wasn't saying so. But that didn't mean he didn't feel it. One thing she had learnt about Jack this weekend was that, despite his outward charm and friendliness, his deeper emotions were something he kept completely to himself.

Please let Harry be all right, she silently pleaded. Because if he wasn't, Mattie had a feeling Jack would never forgive either her or her mother!

'Mich—the vet is in the kitchen with Harry now,' her mother told Jack as she came out of the house to meet them, obviously having been looking out of the window waiting for them to arrive.

Jack nodded tersely. 'I'll go and speak to him.' He strode away without so much as a second glance in Mattie's direction.

He was deeply worried about Harry, Mattie knew that, but nevertheless she felt slightly bereft at his departure. She hadn't realized, until that moment, after spending the last two days in Jack's company, just how difficult it was going to be for her when he went out of her life.

'I'm really sorry about this, Mattie.' Her mother

squeezed her arm in apology. 'But I'm sure you appreciate that I had to let Jack know.'

'Of course you did,' Mattie roused herself enough to reassure her mother. 'Jack would never have forgiven either of us if— How is Harry really?' She frowned her concern.

'Well, he is slightly better this morning,' her mother said cautiously. 'And I'm sure that seeing Jack will cheer him up!'

It would certainly cheer Mattie up if Jack were to visit when she was feeling ill! Not that she ever was ill, she realized disconsolately; she seemed to have one of those healthy constitutions that meant she rarely even got a cold, let alone any other ailments.

'How did your weekend go?' her mother asked curiously, linking her arm companionably with Mattie's. 'Have you had a good time?'

'Very good.' Mattie sighed wistfully. 'Jack's family is—well, they're all really nice.'

Her mother smiled. 'What did you expect? Jack's a nice man.'

Yes, he was. Very nice. Very kind, very charming, very handsome. And Mattie loved him so much she ached with it. But none of that changed the fact that he was soon going to walk out of her life and not look back…

'Where are the dogs?' It didn't seem quite right without the four dogs jumping up and down excitedly.

'I've moved them all into the large back pen while Harry is in the house. I wasn't sure at first whether Harry was contagious, although the vet has assured me he isn't. I've left them there now so that they aren't too boisterous around Harry.'

'I'll pop round and say hello to them all later,' Mattie confirmed. 'I think we had better go inside now and see what the vet has to say,' she said. 'Although I'm pretty sure Jack will want to take Harry home with him.'

She was right. Jack and the vet—a tall, dark-haired man of about fifty—were discussing exactly that as Mattie and her mother joined them.

Mattie left the two men to their conversation, going down on her knees beside the dog basket where Harry lay looking very sorry for himself.

He looked up at her with pale blue eyes. Reproachful eyes, for having taken his master away from him? Or was it just her imagination?

Whatever, it had the desired effect, Mattie instantly feeling as guilty as she was sure Jack must. Maybe if they hadn't left Harry here and gone off to Paris together—

'—pretty sure Harry had the infection for several days before you brought him here,' the vet was explaining softly to Jack. 'And Mrs Crawford acted very quickly and called me in immediately she became aware that Harry was far from well.'

Well at least that let her mother off the hook, Mattie realized with relief. Although it didn't alter the fact that Harry obviously wasn't very well; he certainly wasn't the bouncy excitable dog they had left here two days ago.

'I really would prefer it if you didn't move Harry until tomorrow at the earliest,' the vet continued evenly. 'I would like to call round again first thing in the morning just to make sure he's continuing to improve. If he is, I see no further problem to your taking Harry home.'

'You're quite welcome to stay here tonight, Jack,' Mattie's mother put in practically.

Mattie stared at her. Jack stay here tonight? But—

'I wouldn't want to inconvenience you any more than I already have, Diana.' Jack shook his head.

'You won't be,' Diana assured him briskly. 'You can sleep in Mattie's bedroom.'

Mattie's eyes widened. Surely her mother wasn't suggesting—

'I have a double bed, Mattie can quite easily come in with me,' her mother added with a reproachful look in Mattie's direction that clearly said, I accept that you've been to Paris with Jack for the weekend, but this is our home, remember?

Ah.

Mattie became very interested in talking softly to Harry, her hair falling forward to hide the brightness of her cheeks, desperately hoping that neither of the two men had noticed that look that had passed between her mother and herself. But for a moment she really had thought—

'Is that going to be okay with you, Mattie?' Jack prompted gruffly.

She looked up abruptly. 'Of course,' she confirmed sharply.

'In that case, Diana, I accept your offer. And thank you.' Jack smiled grimly.

'I'll walk you to your car,' Diana told the vet as he closed up his bag ready for departure.

Leaving Mattie and Jack alone in the kitchen...

Jack came down on his haunches next to Harry's basket, reaching out to gently stroke him. 'I hope you weren't just being polite about having to give up your bedroom for me tonight…?'

Mattie glanced at him, wondering if he could have seen that startled look she'd given her mother earlier at her suggestion, after all. But his attention was on Harry, his expression unreadable.

'Not at all,' she dismissed as she straightened up. 'It's the least we can do.' It also meant that she could be with Jack for a little longer.

Jack nodded, also standing up. 'I'll go and get our things from the car. Thanks for being so—understanding, last night and today, Mattie. I appreciate it.' He touched her arm in gentle thanks on his way outside.

Mattie was glad of these few moments of solitude to try to get her chaotic thoughts under control. Whatever had happened between herself and Jack in Paris—and she still had no idea what that was!—it was over. They were back in the real world now, and her real world didn't include Jack. And the sooner she accepted that, the better!

Although that wasn't too easy to do with Jack actually staying in her home overnight!

The three of them sat down together for their evening meal, her mother suggesting they play cards once everything had been cleared away. It was her mother's way of keeping Jack occupied, Mattie knew, but it also meant she was constantly in his company too. Which, in the circumstances, her heightened senses aware of every move Jack made, wasn't easy.

'We're very competitive in my family,' Jack said apologetically as he once again beat the two women at whist.

Jack's family… Mattie had come to like all of his

immediate relatives during this weekend, the heaviness settling on her chest as she realized she wouldn't be seeing any of them again, either.

'I always wanted a large family,' her mother said wistfully. 'But it wasn't to be.'

'It isn't too late for that, surely?' Jack teased as he shuffled the cards.

'Oh, I think at forty-three I'm a little old to even think of having any more children,' Mattie's mother protested, her cheeks a delicate shade of pink.

'Not at all,' Jack dismissed. 'What do you think, Mattie?'

She blinked at the suddenness of what seemed to be a teasing conversation being switched to her. What did she think of her mother having more children? In all honesty, it wasn't something she had ever given any thought to. For the obvious reason her mother had never even dated during the last twenty years.

'She's speechless at the mere suggestion of it.' Her mother laughed, her cheeks still a blushing pink. 'And rightly so.'

'No, I—I'm not speechless,' Mattie said slowly. Her mother was still a young woman, and lots of women her mother's age were having children nowadays. 'It might be rather fun, at that,' she opined.

'You see, Diana.' Jack grinned. 'Mattie wouldn't mind at all.'

Mattie frowned as she looked at the two of them, her mother looking slightly shy now.

Diana gave a firm shake of her head. 'I'm far too old to even think about night feeds and nappies all over again!'

'I didn't get that impression earlier—'

'Are you this much of a tease with your family, Jack?' her mother cut in, standing up as she did so.

'Worse,' he confirmed with another grin.

Diana shook her head. 'Then I'm surprised you lived past puberty! Anyway, it's time the old folk went for their beauty sleep,' she added self-derisively. 'I'll see you in the morning, Jack. Mattie, I'll leave it to you to show Jack where he's to sleep.' She smiled before leaving to go to her bedroom.

Mattie stood up too, the mention of where Jack was to sleep once again throwing her into confusion. 'I hope you won't be too cramped in my bedroom,' she said awkwardly, remembering the luxury of the suite the two of them had just shared in Paris. A luxury Jack was obviously accustomed to...

In contrast, her bedroom was still pretty much as it had been when she was a teenager: pink and white in décor, the books on the shelves definitely juvenile. But at least the posters of pop groups that had once adorned the walls had been taken down a couple of years ago!

'I'm sure I'll be fine,' Jack responded, looking up at her quizzically. 'Though this isn't quite the way I had envisaged us spending this evening!'

Mattie shrugged. 'It doesn't matter. Can I get you a coffee or anything before you go to bed?' She frowned. 'We probably have some whisky somewhere left over from Christmas if you would prefer—'

'No, I'm fine, thanks, Mattie,' he refused, getting up to stretch tiredly. 'At least Harry looks a little happier than when we arrived this afternoon,' he observed. The dog had sat at his feet most of the evening, but rose now to wag his tail at mention of his name.

'Yes,' Mattie bent to tickle Harry behind one floppy

ear. 'I'm glad,' she added with relief; surely Jack would never have forgiven Mattie and her mother if anything had happened to his beloved dog.

Jack gave a rueful shake of his head as he looked down affectionately at his recovering pet. 'Do you think he was part of the conspiracy?' He laughed softly.

The conspiracy to stop Mattie and Jack being alone together...

Mattie gave Harry a considering look. 'He looks intelligent—but I doubt deviousness is part of his character!' she concluded.

'You're right—it isn't!' Jack agreed as he reached out to gently put his arms about Mattie's waist and pull her close against him. 'It appears I still owe you a weekend in Paris,' he murmured huskily. 'After all,' he added before Mattie could speak, 'you kept your part of the bargain.'

Her part of the bargain had been to keep Sharon Keswick at bay—and she had hardly succeeded in doing that!

Mattie couldn't quite meet the warmth of Jack's gaze, very aware of the close proximity of their bodies. 'Your family were very disappointed that you had to leave so suddenly—'

'That *we* had to leave so suddenly,' Jack corrected, having telephoned his parents earlier this evening and assured them that Harry was recovering rapidly. 'My mother likes you very much.'

'That's very kind of her,' Mattie returned noncommittally, even as her cheeks warmed with pleasure.

'Mattie...?'

She looked up at him, the sudden tears in her eyes making her vision slightly unfocused. But not too unfocused that she wasn't aware of Jack bending his head slightly, his mouth gently exploring against hers.

But it wasn't gentle for long, Mattie unsure which one of them had deepened the kiss, only knowing herself suddenly swept along on a tide of longing as Jack's mouth moved fiercely against hers.

He felt so wonderful against her, so—so absolutely male, his chest warm beneath her fingertips. Whereas her breasts had hardened at Jack's lightest touch, Mattie groaning low in her throat as his thumbtips caressed those fiery tips, the warmth in her thighs spreading over her whole body, her skin sensitized to his every move.

Jacks's lips moved down the arched column of her throat now, Mattie gasping her pleasure as those lips claimed one bared breast, the nipple hard against the soft rasping of his tongue.

Mattie had never known such mindless desire, such complete and utter pleasure, knew herself lost, wanted nothing more than to lie down and let herself be taken—

'No!' She came sharply to her senses, pulling away from him, stepping back to straighten her dishevelled clothes, unable to meet the heat of his gaze. 'The weekend is over, Jack,' she said hardly. 'And—this, certainly wasn't part of our deal,' she added firmly.

'But—'

'It's been a very long and emotional weekend, Jack, and even if you aren't tired, I am,' she told him bluntly, unable to actually look at him again. Because she was afraid of what might happen if she did!

'I *am* tired, Mattie,' he began slowly.

'Good,' she bit out tersely. 'If you would like to get your bag, I'll show you where you're to sleep.'

She didn't wait to see Jack pick up his case from the

corner of the kitchen where he had dropped it earlier, turning to go out into the hallway to walk to her bedroom at the back of the bungalow. But, nevertheless, she was completely aware of Jack walking behind her down the carpeted hallway, could feel the darkness of his gaze burning down the length of her spine.

But she daredn't turn and acknowledge that gaze, knew that at that moment they were both walking along a very fine edge between desire and reason. And that for both their sakes reason had to win!

'Sorry about the décor.' She grimaced as she opened her bedroom door and showed him inside, very conscious of how feminine the room was, made more so by Jack's complete masculinity.

'It's fine,' Jack assured her distractedly.

It was far from fine, Jack looking completely incongruous as he sat down on the pink and white lace on her bed, a dozen or so dolls from her childhood arranged on the ottoman at its foot.

'The bathroom is outside, first door on the right.' The awkwardness of that sudden earlier desire between them made her voice terse.

Jack looked up and smiled at her. 'Thanks.'

Mattie still stood awkwardly by the open door. 'I'll see you in the morning, then,' she said quietly before turning away.

'Mattie…?'

She swallowed hard, stiffening her shoulders as she slowly turned back to face him. 'Yes?'

His head tilted quizzically to one side, a perplexed frown on his face. 'I— Earlier wasn't the first time I've kissed you.'

It was the first time she had lost control so completely!
'I know that,' she responded impatiently.

'I didn't mean for things to go so far just now. It's just…' He paused. 'You're…different, somehow, since we got back to England.'

'Different'! Of course she was different. Before they'd gone away she had found him attractive, enjoyed his company, quite enjoyed their verbal sparring, too, but during the last two days she had fallen in love with him. Of course she was different!

'I don't know what you mean,' she denied sharply praying silently that she hadn't given her feelings away so completely!

But Jack persisted. 'You seem—distant, not at all the feisty Mattie I've come to know this last week.'

'I told you—I'm tired.'

Jack seemed unconvinced. 'And that's all it is?'

'Of course.' Her gaze was fixed on the rosebud wallpaper just above his shoulder. 'I'm sure we'll all be feeling a lot brighter after a good night's sleep,' she added offhandedly.

Jack nodded slowly, obviously still not satisfied with her reply, but not about to push for an answer any further this evening. 'In that case, I'll wish you goodnight.'

'Goodnight,' she echoed softly, closing the door behind her as she left the room.

Mattie hesitated in the hallway outside, very aware of the fact that she needed to be alone for a few minutes before going to the bedroom she was to share with her mother. The two of them had always been very close, but the love Mattie felt towards Jack was still too raw to share with anyone, even her mother.

Harry looked up briefly from his basket as she re-entered the kitchen, turning away disinterestedly when he saw it was only Mattie.

Mattie knew how he felt!

'Sorry, boy,' she murmured as she sat down at the kitchen table to look at the disappointed dog. 'I guess we both love Jack, and only Jack, hmm?'

But how could love be like this? Painful as much as pleasurable? Pleasure in everything Jack did or said, in just being in the same room as him, let alone the ecstasy of being in his arms. But along with that the pain of knowing that he could never return the feelings she had for him.

At last she gave in to the tears that had been threatening for so long. Hot, uncontrollable tears that made her whole body tremble as she grieved for the loss of the man who had never been hers to start with, a man she had to let walk out of her life tomorrow without him ever guessing that Mattie loved him.

How could she bear it?

How…!

CHAPTER TWELVE

'GOOD morning!' Mattie greeted brightly as Jack came into the kitchen at eight o'clock the next morning. 'Would you like a full English breakfast, or just cereal and toast?' she offered even as she poured him a mug of strong coffee from the percolator.

This was how she bore it, she had decided in the early hours of this morning as she'd lain awake in the huge double bed beside her sleeping mother.

Jack seemed to want bright and cheerful, so bright and cheerful was what she was going to get. There would be plenty of time for tears later, Mattie had decided firmly. Once Jack had gone…

Jack winced, looking less than bright himself, dark smudges beneath his eyes, the dark shadow on his jawline proof that he hadn't shaved yet, seeming to have pulled on only a shirt and denims before coming through to the kitchen, his feet bare. 'Nothing else but the coffee just now, thanks.' He took a grateful sip of the strong brew. 'Where's Harry?' He looked around the deserted kitchen.

'He went for a walk with my mother,' Mattie reported happily. 'He's obviously feeling much better this morning,' she added with satisfaction.

'As are you,' Jack observed, still not quite awake as he blinked at her owlishly.

'I told you I would be,' Mattie returned.

'Are you always this cheerful in the morning?'

'Pretty much,' Mattie agreed, putting some bread in the toaster anyway. No doubt Jack would eat it if she prepared it; they certainly hadn't eaten much yesterday, having had nothing before they'd left the hotel, Jack having had little appetite for the dinner she and her mother had prepared last night, either.

Jack strolled over to the open kitchen door, looking outside at the early morning sunshine. 'The weather seems to be reflecting your mood,' he said.

Which was more than could be said for him!

Mattie chuckled. 'Are you always this grumpy in the morning?' After all, this was the first time she had seen him after a night's sleep, too; Saturday morning he had already left for the airport when she'd got up, and yesterday morning they had been up all night anyway!

He glanced back at her. 'Pretty much,' he dryly repeated her own reply of a few seconds ago, strolling back into the kitchen.

She gave a rueful shake of her head. 'Just as well we don't live together all the time, then, isn't it?' she retorted, putting the toast on the table with the butter and preserves already there.

'Mattie—'

'Would you like a refill on the coffee?' she cut in busily. 'Just help yourself if you do.' She indicated the full percolator of coffee on the side. 'I'm just going outside to see if my mother needs any help.' She hurried out of the kitchen before Jack had chance to make any reply.

Keep it up, she told herself firmly as she walked quickly round to where the kennels were.

With any luck Jack would be gone in an hour or so, and then she could give in to the misery she was really feeling. But until that time Jack would continue to get the full force of the preferred bright and cheerful Mattie Crawford.

Her mother wasn't so easily fooled, giving her a searching glance as Mattie joined her in the kennels. 'You were late coming to bed last night. I heard Jack come to bed hours before you did,' she continued as Mattie would have replied.

Successfully preventing Mattie from inventing the excuse of a long conversation with Jack having delayed her!

'I just wasn't sleepy. All the excitement of the weekend, I expect.' Mattie said.

'Michael has already called—Michael Vaughan. The vet,' her mother explained at Mattie's blank look. 'He called in a few minutes ago on his way to his surgery. He says that, as Harry seems pretty much back to normal, he can go home with Jack this morning.' Her mother sighed her relief as they both turned to watch Harry in the large outside pen, Sophie happily ensconced in there with him. 'They're great friends,' Diana added happily.

'So I see,' Mattie agreed; if Sophie's—excuse the pun!—dog-like devotion was anything to go by, then Jack's charm had spilt over onto his pet!

Her mother gave her another sideways glance. 'Have you seen Jack yet this morning?' she asked casually.

Too casually, for Mattie's liking. Had her mother guessed how she felt about Jack? And, if her mother could so easily see how she felt about him, could Jack see it too?

That would be just too humiliating!

'He's eating breakfast,' Mattie replied just as casually,

collecting up the bowls ready for feeding. 'I'll go and do this, shall I?' She didn't wait for her mother's answer, hurrying off to the room at the back of the office where they prepared the food.

Just another hour or so, Mattie, she told herself encouragingly. And then the only time she might possibly catch a glimpse of Jack would be when she went to his offices to care for the plants, and the flowers in Reception; as she had never caught a glimpse of him before on any of her visits there, that wasn't very likely!

She took her time over preparing the food and delivering it to their guests, the dogs setting up a cacophony of noise at the mere suggestion of breakfast.

'How on earth do you hear yourself think?'

Mattie's hands shook, and she almost dropped the bowl of food she was carrying, at the unexpected sound of Jack's voice. She schooled her features into neutrality before turning to smile at him. 'You don't,' she answered loudly, her breath catching in her throat at his newly shaved and showered appearance, the creased tee shirt and denims he had worn earlier replaced with an obviously laundered shirt and smart black denims. He was also wearing shoes. 'Harry is round the back with Sophie if you're looking for him. The vet has already been, and declared him fit for home,' she explained before turning away.

'Mattie.'

He hadn't gone yet!

She turned back slowly. 'I'll be finished here shortly,' she said.

Jack looked at her consideringly. 'Come and have a cup of coffee with me before I leave,' he prompted.

And talk about what? The wonderful weekend they

had spent together? What had happened between them last night. How they must do this again some time? Mattie didn't think so!

The fact was they would never see each other again, and Mattie had never particularly liked goodbyes; this one promised to be more painful than most.

She gave a shake of her head. 'I'm going in to my shop as soon as I've finished here,' she told him.

Jack frowned. 'But it's a bank holiday.'

Mattie nodded. 'But I have mail and—and things, to check up on, before I open up again tomorrow. I'm sure you know how it is when you're in business, Jack,' she offered, knowing full well that her little business in no way compared with the multimillion pound JB Industries.

'Even I take holidays, Mattie,' he countered.

'Because you aren't more or less a one-man band,' she reasoned. 'Do go and see Harry,' she encouraged. 'He really is so much better.'

'Coffee,' Jack bit out determinedly. 'In ten minutes,' he added firmly before walking away.

Yes, sir. No, sir. Right away, sir, Mattie fumed at his retreating back.

'Was that Jack I heard just now?' her mother questioned interestedly as she came out of the kennel she had been cleaning.

Mattie nodded, turning away from glaring in the direction Jack had so recently disappeared. 'He's leaving shortly,' she confirmed.

Her mother gave her a rueful glance. 'Cheer up, Mattie.' She gave an encouraging squeeze of her daughter's arm. 'I'm sure you'll be seeing him again soon.'

Mattie drew in a sharp breath before giving a shake

of her head. 'Mum, I hate to disappoint you, but, after the awful weekend I've just spent with him, I really don't care if I never set eyes on Jack Beauchamp ever again,' she admitted.

She didn't want to see Jack again! Soon or otherwise! Seeing him just made the ache in her heart all the more unbearable!

But why did her mother look so stricken? Surely she was the one who—

'That's rather a pity, Mattie,' Jack spoke icily from just behind her. 'Because I know for a fact my mother has every intention of sending you an invitation to Sandy and Thom's wedding.'

Mattie gave a pained grimace, unable to look at her mother, even as she sensed Diana's sympathy. But how could she possibly have guessed that Jack would return so quickly from collecting Harry and overhear her last, scathing remark?

A Harry who was even now jumping around her feet, the attentive Sophie at his side.

But even if Mattie had seen the two dogs, she still couldn't have known that Jack was close enough to overhear her last statement. Her last damning statement!

She turned slowly, feeling her face pale slightly at the unmistakable disappointment she could see on Jack's face. Well, what had he expected—a Mattie as totally besotted with him as the overwhelming Sharon Keswick? No way would she ever make such a public fool of herself over Jack, or any other man, in the way that the other woman had all weekend. In fact, Jack was the one who had said it was Sharon Keswick's clinginess that had put him off the other woman in the first place!

She shrugged dismissively. 'I'm sure that I can come

up with a feasible excuse for not being there,' she answered evenly. 'After all, your mother will only be sending the invitation because she believes the two of us are friends.' And Jack couldn't really want her there, either!

Jack's mouth tightened, his expression grim. 'Something we obviously aren't,' he rasped.

'Of course we're friends, Jack,' she said impatiently, furious with herself and Jack, she for having made that reckless statement in the first place about never wanting to see him again, and Jack, because he had overheard it. Not very logical, she knew, but then logic just didn't come into her feelings where Jack was concerned. 'Just not the sort of friends your mother believes we are,' she added reasoningly.

Jack looked at her silently for several long seconds, his enigmatic gaze giving away none of what he was thinking.

Perhaps it was as well not to know exactly what that was, Mattie consoled herself; she had no doubt that, charming as he was, Jack could have a rapier tongue if he chose to use it. And, after her damning statement of a few minutes ago, he no doubt thought Mattie deserved it!

He gave an abrupt inclination of his head before turning towards her mother. 'Time I was going, I think, Diana,' he said. 'I've imposed on your hospitality quite long enough.' His voice hardened perceptibly.

'Not at all,' her mother hastened to reassure him, shooting Mattie a reproving look as she walked past her to join Jack at the door. 'Come and have a cup of coffee before you go,' she encouraged warmly.

'Thanks for the offer, Diana, but I really think it's best if I go now,' Jack refused.

So much for the cup of coffee he had suggested—ordered!—Mattie to have with him a few minutes ago. Not that she wanted to sit and have coffee with him, but now that it was actually time for him to go she didn't want him to.

Jack turned slightly in her direction. 'Goodbye, Mattie,' he added with hard finality.

Mattie drew in a deeply controlling breath before answering him, determined not to show how devastated she felt at the thought of him leaving, of him walking out of her life for ever. ''Bye, Jack,' she returned with a lightness she was far from feeling. 'Take care,' she added impulsively, wishing there were something she could say to stop him leaving, but inwardly knowing she had already said enough—more than enough!

He nodded abruptly. 'You, too.'

'Yes,' she acknowledged breathlessly, unable to look at him any more, turning away to studiously start filling water bowls as the tears stung her eyes, threatening to fall and betray how she really felt about Jack leaving.

'Mattie? Mattie, aren't you coming to see Jack off?' her mother prompted in sharp rebuke.

A well-deserved rebuke, Mattie knew; her behaviour must seem incredibly rude to her mother when she and Jack had just spent the weekend in Paris together. But there was no way Mattie could stand beside her mother in the driveway and wave Jack a fond farewell without making that public fool of herself she so much wanted to avoid!

She blinked back the tears, stiffening her shoulders in resolve; she would not behave like an idiot and begin to cry. Not until after Jack had gone, at any rate!

'I'm sure it doesn't take two of us to wave Jack good-bye,' she derided.

Her mother looked absolutely horrified at this continuing display of bad manners, Mattie easily able to feel the sharp sting of her mother's disappointment. But if she backed down now then her mother might be even more disappointed in her behaviour; Mattie would look most undignified clinging to Jack's ankles as she begged him not to leave!

'Don't worry about it, Diana.' Jack was the one to speak harshly as her mother would have spoken. 'Mattie assures me she is very busy today.' Too busy to even take the time to properly say goodbye, his tone implied.

'I'll be in tomorrow evening as usual to see to the plants.' The awkwardness of the situation compelled Mattie to say something.

Jack gave a mocking inclination of his head. 'I'm sure the plants will appreciate that,' he replied. 'Come on, Harry,' he called to his dog as he turned away.

'What on earth is wrong with you, Mattie?' her mother lingered long enough to hiss.

Mattie shook her head wordlessly, staring miserably after Jack as he walked off with long, measured strides. There was simply nothing she could say, nothing she could do, to alter the fact that Jack was walking out of her life for good.

'I think you and I need to talk when I come back,' her mother told her quickly before hurrying off to join Jack.

All the talk in the world couldn't change the fact that Mattie was in love with a man who didn't love her, who would never love her.

Nothing could change that.

But as she heard the slam of Jack's car door, quickly followed by the start of the car engine, Mattie knew she couldn't just stand here after all, her feet moving automatically as she began to run towards the front of the house, knowing that she had to at least have one last glance at Jack as he drove away.

She arrived on the driveway just in time to see Jack accelerate the car down the driveway, lifting her hand in wan salute, even as she knew he probably couldn't even see her there, the prick of tears burning her eyes now.

'I'm glad you changed your mind.' Her mother linked her arm with Mattie's as she moved to stand beside her, squeezing reassuringly.

Mattie couldn't speak, completely choked with the tears she knew were going to fall. There was no way she could stop them a moment longer—

'Mum, there are two dogs in the back of Jack's car!' she suddenly realized, two canine faces against the back window, two healthy pink tongues pressed against the glass.

Her mother nodded, smiling warmly. 'Jack has taken Sophie with him.'

Mattie shook her head dazedly. 'But—'

'He asked if he could have her that morning he came to see me,' her mother explained happily.

Mattie blinked. 'He did?' Had that been the subject of Jack's discussion with her mother that morning? Besides assuring her mother that he didn't have designs on her baby's body!

Her mother confirmed it. 'Apparently you had told him Sophie's sad story, and, after thinking about it for a few days, he knew he couldn't bear the thought of her being abandoned in that way. That's the reason Sophie and Harry have spent so much time together these last few days, to see if they would get on together.'

Mattie could only stare after the fast-disappearing car.

Jack had taken Sophie home with him.

How Mattie wished that she could have been the one he took home with him!

CHAPTER THIRTEEN

'Come on, Mattie,' her mother encouraged once the red sports car had disappeared completely from view. 'You and I are going to have a chat over a cup of coffee.'

Mattie grimaced her reluctance. 'If the conversation is going to have anything concerning Jack in it—'

'It's all going to have Jack in it,' her mother cut in firmly.

'Then I would like to postpone it for a while,' Mattie answered determinedly, knowing she really did need some time alone. 'Only until this afternoon, Mum,' she encouraged as her mother would have protested. 'You still have some work to do here, and I—I would just like to go and check that everything is okay at the shop.' She used the same excuse as she had with Jack minutes ago.

Her mother, however, didn't look convinced; in fact she looked as if she would like to argue this last point. But one look at Mattie's face and she seemed to change her mind. 'Okay,' she agreed. 'This afternoon it is, then. But no longer than that,' she warned. 'I wasn't at all sure when the two of you got back yesterday, couldn't tell—' She shook her head. 'You're simply making yourself miserable for nothing, Mattie.' She sighed frustratedly.

Mattie wouldn't exactly call falling in love with Jack nothing. But her mother was probably right; she should never have fallen in love with him in the first place.

She gave another grimace. 'I'll get over it.'

Her mother raised blonde brows. 'Somehow I doubt that,' she murmured.

So did Mattie, but hearing her mother echo those sentiments certainly didn't help!

'I'll be back in time for lunch,' Mattie assured Diana, turning towards the bungalow to go and collect her bag and car keys.

'Make sure you are,' her mother warned. 'Oh, and Mattie…'

She turned back with a frown. 'Yes?'

Her mother looked slightly embarrassed now, her gaze not quite meeting Mattie's. 'I—er—I won't be in for dinner this evening.' The words came out in a rush. 'I—er—I'm going out,' she concluded flatly.

Mattie looked searchingly at her mother. Her beautiful mother, she acknowledged slowly, Diana's eyes sparkling brightly, attractive colour in her cheeks as she still looked embarrassed.

Ah.

But whom—? 'Michael Vaughan looks a very nice man,' she said casually, knowing she had made the right guess as her mother's cheeks became even redder.

'Er—yes,' Diana conceded awkwardly. 'He's a widower. His wife died two years ago. And we have our love of animals in common. He's asked me out several times before, but I—'

'Always said no,' Mattie realized. 'It's all right, Mum,' she said laughingly as her mother looked more and more uncomfortable by the second. 'As I said, he looks nice. And you're certainly beautiful enough.'

'Don't be silly,' her mother dismissed, although her eyes shone with pleasure now at Mattie's positive reaction. 'You know, I've been dreading telling you,' she admitted.

'I can't imagine why,' Mattie returned, moving to kiss her mother warmly on the cheek. 'It's about time the male population woke up and realized how beautiful you are!'

Her mother shook her head. 'I think you may be biased, Mattie.'

'Well, if I can't be biased, who can?' She hugged her mother. 'I can't wait to hear all the details later,' she encouraged.

'There aren't any details,' her mother called after her in protest.

'Yet,' Mattie turned briefly to tease.

'Oh, go on with you,' her mother said crossly, although the smile on her face contradicted the emotion.

Mattie kept herself busy at the shop for the rest of the morning, checking her mail and the orders for tomorrow, and generally tidying up. It didn't stop her from thinking of Jack, from missing him, but it helped to keep the tears at bay. There was—

She frowned at the telephone as it began to ring; she shouldn't even be here today, let alone expect any orders to come in. Oh, well, she was here, and an order was an order.

'Green and Beautiful,' she announced into the receiver. 'How may I help you?'

'The last sentiment I agree with, although I don't think the first one suits you at all,' Jack came back sardonically. 'But there is a way you can help me, Mattie.'

Mattie froze, her hand tightly gripping the receiver. Jack. It was Jack. The very last person she had expected to hear from ever again.

'Mattie?' he pressed concernedly several seconds later at her lack of a reply.

She couldn't move, couldn't speak, her face pale as she tried to make sense of this unexpected call. She had told Jack she was going to the shop, but she certainly hadn't thought he would get in touch with her here!

'Mattie, are you still there? Mattie? Damn it, the line's gone dead,' Jack muttered to himself impatiently.

'No, it hasn't!' Mattie burst out forcefully before he could break the connection. 'I just—I wasn't expecting you to call, that's all.' That was all!

She had spent most of the morning quietly grieving for the man she loved, expecting never to see or hear from him again, and a few hours later he telephoned her! She was in shock, that was what she was.

'No. Well. I probably wouldn't have called you today if—well, I have something of an emergency, Mattie,' he admitted.

'Is there something wrong with Sophie?' She instantly panicked. 'And why didn't you tell me you were taking her?' she continued disgruntledly. 'We were together for three days, and you never mentioned a word. I—'

'No, it isn't Sophie,' Jack answered her calmly. 'She's absolutely fine, perfect company for Harry. And I didn't tell you over the weekend that I would be taking Sophie when we got back because, quite frankly, we had lots of other things to talk about.'

Such as Sharon Keswick. Such as his having four sisters and not four girlfriends, as she had originally thought. Such as—

'Mattie, my parents returned to England this morning, and my mother rang half an hour ago and invited the two of us over for dinner this evening,' Jack interrupted her increasingly angry thoughts.

'And that's the reason you're telephoning me?' Mattie returned disbelievingly.

'Yes. You see—'

'No, Jack,' Mattie cut in determinedly. 'The answer is definitely no!'

'Why?' he demanded.

'Well, one of the reasons is that I've only just got back from spending the weekend with you—' she began.

'Your mother is going out this evening, so don't try to use spending time with her as your excuse for refusing,' Jack interjected.

Mattie gasped. 'How did you know—?'

'I called the house before calling you at the shop, and during the course of our conversation Diana told me she would be out this evening,' Jack explained patiently. 'Besides which, it was pretty obvious yesterday that the vet liked—more than liked—Diana,' he added reasoningly.

Mattie couldn't say she had noticed, but then her head had been pretty full of thoughts of Jack yesterday to notice much else...

'Okay, so my mother is going out,' she conceded. 'But I'm still surprised that a man like you could even suggest the two of us have dinner with your parents this evening.'

Under other circumstances, she would have jumped at the chance of seeing Jack again, for whatever reason. But she had genuinely liked his parents, his mother in particular had been very kind to her over the weekend, and this act she and Jack had perpetrated had already gone on long enough, as far as Mattie was concerned.

'Look, I appreciate that you made your feelings towards me quite clear earlier,' Jack answered. 'But I was under the impression that you liked my parents—'

'I do!' she put in hurriedly. 'That's the reason I'm not going with you to have dinner with them this evening. Jack, the weekend was one thing.' She sighed. 'But it's over now, and you owe it to your parents to tell them the truth about—about us,' she said haltingly. 'I, for one, wouldn't feel happy continuing to deceive them in that way—and I don't think you should, either!'

Silence on the other end of the telephone line followed her outburst.

But what else could she do or say? She simply couldn't go on pretending that she and Jack were a couple—not when it was what she most wanted in the world, and knew would never happen.

'Jack?' she queried anxiously seconds later at his continued silence.

'You said a few minutes ago that you were surprised that a man like me…' Jack answered slowly. 'Exactly what sort of man do you think I am, Mattie?'

The sort of man she had fallen in love with! Loyal. Kind. Loving. Family orientated. Add to that the facts that he was also handsome, sexy, and incredibly charming, and what chance had Mattie had not to fall in love with him?

'The sort that wouldn't continue to act the deliberate lie, that our relationship is, to his parents,' she claimed softly.

'Mattie…' Jack's voice was gentle. '…as far as I'm concerned, it isn't an act.'

'I just can't do it any more, Jack!' she groaned. 'I really like your parents, and— What did you just say?'

She stopped suddenly, becoming very still as his words penetrated the misery that had surrounded her all morning.

'It isn't an act on my part, Mattie,' he repeated evenly.

'But—'

'It never has been,' Jack said.

Mattie swallowed very hard, all the colour fading from her cheeks, suddenly feeling hot and cold at the same time, her breath so shallow it was barely perceptible. Jack couldn't really have just said— Could he…?

'It's okay, Mattie,' Jack cut heavily into her frozen silence. 'I'm not expecting you to make any declarations of love back—as I said earlier, you made your feelings towards me more than clear this morning. But I—'

'Jack,' she interjected, her hand slippery with heat as she tightly gripped the telephone receiver, her legs feeling shaky, 'I don't think this is the sort of conversation we should be having over the phone—'

'Well, after this morning, I'm certainly not about to tell you any of this to your face,' Jack assured her. 'You know, I never knew until this morning how painful rejection could be. I'm almost thirty-three years old, you know, Mattie, and it never bothered me that I had so far not met the woman I wanted to spend the rest of my life with. You can't know this, but my parents fell in love with each other at first sight, and I always expected that's how it would happen with me. Well, it did,' he concluded dryly. 'I just hadn't taken into account the fact that the woman I fell in love with at first sight wouldn't feel the same way about me!'

But she did! She was just so stunned by Jack's admission that she couldn't speak!

Jack *loved* her? Had fallen in love with her at first sight? The same way she had fallen in love with him…

Jack gave a sad sigh. 'I appreciate what you're saying about dinner with my parents this evening, Mattie. It was a bad idea. A desperate move by a desperate man,' he conceded. 'I'll explain to my parents, tell them what was really happening over the weekend. My mother will just have to live with the disappointment of not seeing you again. As will I,' he pronounced flatly.

'I—but—no!' Mattie finally managed to speak—at the same time knowing she sounded like a bumbling idiot. She was just so stunned. So shocked. So *euphoric*. Jack loved her! She didn't need to know anything else.

'No?' he repeated uncertainly.

'I think dinner this evening with your parents sounds a wonderful idea,' she told him breathlessly. 'I—it wasn't—isn't an act on my part, either, Jack,' she added quickly.

Before she lost her nerve! Pride was one thing—it was what had driven her to make that damning statement this morning, after all. But Jack had been totally honest with her; she owed him the same honesty in return. She didn't owe it to him—she gladly gave it to him! Besides, hadn't Thom warned her that he had lost Sandy five years ago because he'd been too stupid to tell her how he felt about her? Mattie didn't want to make the same mistake with Jack!

'Mattie…?' The uncertainty could still be heard in Jack's voice.

Proof enough—if she needed any!—that Jack was telling her the truth when he said he had fallen in love with her at first sight; he was the least uncertain person she had ever met in her life!

'Could we talk about this—face to face, do you think?' she suggested nervously. 'A telephone really is the most—the most—'

'Impersonal thing in the world,' Jack finished for her, definitely less uncertain than he had been. 'Don't move, Mattie,' he told her quickly. 'I'm coming right over!'

'I'm not going anywhere,' she assured him emotionally.

Except... Her shop, surrounded by buckets of flowers and artificial arrangements, was hardly the ideal place, either, for the sort of conversation she thought—hoped—the two of them were going to have!

'Jack!' she called desperately before he had chance to end the call.

'Yes?' he replied slowly, sounding uncertain again.

'There's a park across the road from the shop. I—I'll be waiting there for you,' she told him. 'It's such a beautifully warm day, and—'

'As long as you're waiting for me somewhere, Mattie, I don't care where it is!' Jack responded decisively. 'I'll be there in ten minutes,' he promised before ringing off.

Mattie slowly replaced her own receiver, still not quite able to believe what was happening to her. To them. She hadn't misunderstood, had she? Jack really had said he had fallen in love with her at first sight, hadn't he?

Hadn't he...?

CHAPTER FOURTEEN

MATTIE was standing by an ornamental garden, pretending an interest, when she caught sight of Jack striding purposefully towards her from the direction of the south gate, hastily looking away again as she wondered what they were going to say to each other. The telephone might be impersonal, but it was that very impersonality that had made it possible earlier for her to talk to Jack in the way that she had. Face to face like this —

Jack felt no such inhibitions, sweeping her up into his arms the moment he reached her side. 'I love you, Matilda-May Crawford!' he groaned before bending his head, his mouth taking possession of Mattie's in a kiss that allowed no room for doubt as to the truth of his claim.

Jack did love her!

Mattie's arms moved up about his shoulders, her fingers becoming entangled in the dark thickness of his hair as she returned his kiss with all of the love she had bottled up inside her.

Her cheeks were flushed, her eyes fever-bright, by the time Jack raised his head to look down at her with piercing brown eyes.

'Whew!' Jack gave a shake of his head. 'I hope you don't believe in long engagements!'

Mattie moistened her lips. 'Engagements...?' she questioned.

'Engagement. Singular,' he corrected, his arms about

her waist moulding her body against his. 'Ours,' he elaborated decisively—just in case she should be in any doubt as to his meaning! 'I want to marry you, Mattie.' His voice softened emotionally. 'In fact, nothing less than marriage will do,' he stated.

Marriage? But— She hadn't thought that far ahead! Was still trying to come to terms with the fact that Jack claimed to be in love with her!

She shook her head dazedly. 'But you don't even know me,' she protested. 'We've only known each other for—' she did a quick calculation in her head '—for nine days!'

He shrugged. 'I knew how I felt about you after nine *minutes*,' he admitted. 'I took one look at you when I visited the kennels last Sunday, and knew I had finally met the woman I've been searching for all my life,' he said simply.

It had taken her a little longer than that—perhaps ten minutes or so!

'As for knowing each other,' Jack continued, 'we have the rest of our lives together to do that. By the way,' he added lightly, his eyes teasingly dark, 'I should just tell you that I'm not really grumpy in the mornings; I just wasn't too happy this morning because the time was rapidly approaching when I knew I had to say goodbye to you.'

Mattie knew how he'd felt!

Jack looked at her face concernedly, his expression softening to tenderness as he easily saw her shy confusion. 'Let's go and sit on that bench over there,' he suggested gently, his arm lightly about her shoulders now. 'We can tell each other our deepest, darkest secrets. And then I'll ask you to marry me again. Okay?'

Mattie took a deep breath. 'Okay,' she accepted, already knowing what her answer would be; nothing Jack told her about himself could possibly change the fact that she loved him. Absolutely. Completely.

'Do you want me to go first, or would you like to do that?' Jack asked once they were sitting down.

Mattie gave a self-derisive grimace. 'I may as well; it will probably be much shorter than what you have to say!'

He looked at her, arching an eyebrow. 'I'm not sure I care for your inference, Miss Crawford.'

No, in retrospect, it had sounded a little— Well, after all, she knew very little about Jack's personal life before the two of them had met—except for Sharon Keswick, of course, and that didn't seem to have been too successful. But it was wrong of her to assume there had been lots of other women in Jack's life.

'Sorry.' She made a face.

'Apology accepted,' Jack said, eyes gleaming with laughter.

'As for me,' Mattie went on, 'there isn't much to tell. I had a crush on the Maths teacher when I was at school—'

'Male or female?'

'Male, of course.' Mattie frowned in mock reproval. 'Then I had a couple of boyfriends during my university years—'

'How many is a couple?' Jack scowled darkly.

'One or two,' she answered breezily; Jack really cared that there had ever been any other man casually in her life! 'One definitely, because we dated for a couple of months—just dated, Jack,' she assured him hastily as his scowl deepened. 'And the other one... We didn't actually get through the first date together, so I'm not sure he really counts!'

Jack looked quizzical. 'What happened?'

'He seemed to think that buying me a pizza—a pizza, for goodness' sake!—entitled him to sharing my bed for the night. I soon corrected him about that assumption!'

'I'll just bet you did.' Jack chuckled. 'Is that it? No big, dark secrets?'

'Well...' She hesitated briefly. 'I did have a brief relationship last year that ended when the man in question confessed he was already engaged to someone else and the wedding was imminent!'

'Ah,' Jack murmured comprehendingly.

'Ah, indeed,' Mattie agreed. 'No excuse, I know, but—I really am sorry about the mix-up with the cards on your sister's flowers.' She looked at him anxiously.

'No real harm done,' Jack replied. 'And it would have taken me that much longer to meet you without it,' he reasoned.

That was one way of looking at it...

'Your turn,' she invited warmly.

'Hmm.' Jack gave the matter some thought. 'Well, I had a crush on the Games mistress when I was at school. Dated three girls during university—there wasn't the time for any more than that,' he insisted as Mattie looked sceptical. 'Since then...I've had a couple of relationships in the last ten years, but nothing serious, and I've more or less managed to stay friends with both those women. And Sharon you know about,' he admitted. 'I haven't so much as had a date since I went out with her a few years ago; she's the type of woman to cure you of the idea of ever going out with a woman again, let alone having any fun with one!'

Exactly how she had felt after going out with Richard! And Jack really *didn't* like Sharon, Mattie realized happily.

'Until you came along.' Jack smiled.

'There's no doubting you had great fun then—at my expense!' she acknowledged dryly.

He shook his head. 'I think you gave back as good as you got.' He laughed. 'I had got to know you well enough by the evening we had dinner at the Eiffel Tower to think you might stab me with a steak knife, at least, once you learnt the truth about who Tina, Sally, Cally, and Sandy really are!'

'You should have seen the look on your face that night!' Mattie recalled, laughing. 'You were trying so hard to tell me the truth—and being foiled at every turn!'

'Families!' he exclaimed disgustedly.

'I think your family are all lovely,' she defended. 'And, as you've already pointed out, we may not have met at all if it weren't for your sisters,' she reminded him, still embarrassed at the part she had played in that particular situation.

'I'm a great believer in the course of true love. Now, do you think we've told each other enough about our pasts for the moment? Because I really would rather just get to the part where I ask you to marry me,' he told her, taking her hand lightly in both of his, his gaze darkly compelling on the paleness of her face.

Mattie began to tremble all over again, her shyness returning too. 'I—' She stopped, searching for the right words. 'We're so different, Jack—'

'Well, I'm a man, and you're a woman,' he acknowledged. 'But I'm told that's the usual combination in a marriage!'

'You know I didn't mean that.' She sighed shakily.

'I know exactly what you meant.' His hands tightened about hers, his expression serious now. 'I just choose to ignore it. Mattie, surely all that matters is that we love each other? Although, maybe that's the problem…?' he concluded uncertainly. 'Am I taking too much for granted here, Mattie? Don't you—?'

'Of course I love you!' she cut in forcefully, knowing that was going to be his next question. 'I just—'

'Just nothing!' Jack turned fully to pull her fiercely into his arms. 'Mattie, if you want, I can be like Thom, and spend the next five years hanging around in an effort to convince you that I love you—but I would really rather not have to do that,' he told her. 'I want to be with you now. All the time. I want to wake up with you in the morning, have breakfast with you, have lunch with you if that's possible, come home to you every night and have dinner with you before spending our evening together. I want to go to sleep in your arms every night!'

She wanted those things too. So much!

She swallowed hard. 'But won't you—won't you get bored with that after a while?' Bored with *her*!

'Will you?' he returned.

'No,' she answered him honestly, imagining nothing more wonderful than the life together he had just described.

His arms tightened. 'You could never bore me, Mattie; you're far too unpredictable to ever do that.'

She shuddered at the truth of that! 'But what about your family—?'

'What about them?' He frowned.

'Well, won't they think—? They must know we haven't

known each other very long, won't they think all this a bit—sudden?'

Jack shook his head, smiling. 'Mattie, I hate to tell you this, but the fact that you accompanied me to Paris at the weekend told them all exactly where I want our relationship to go. Deliberately so, on my part, I have to admit,' he admitted.

He had known exactly what conclusions his family would come to concerning the two of them! In fact, that seemed to be exactly what he had intended all along...

'In fact, if I know my mother,' Jack continued dryly, 'she'll be going out tomorrow to choose her outfit for the wedding!'

'Hmm,' Mattie acknowledged slowly. 'Talking of mothers...'

'You don't mind that your mother is going out on a date this evening, do you?' Jack said concernedly. 'She's still a lovely woman, you know, Mattie, and—'

'Of course I don't mind,' Mattie assured him sincerely. 'In fact, I couldn't be happier. I've been telling her for years that she ought to go out more, find someone to share the rest of her life with.'

'But you see, Mattie, she would never do that while she had you,' Jack said ruefully.

'I can see that now,' she said. 'Which is why I can't help wondering exactly what it was you said to my mother when you came to see her that morning last week. If I'm not mistaken, it was enough for her to finally agree to go out with Michael Vaughan,' she deduced.

'Hey—' Jack grasped her shoulders '—this hasn't been some huge conspiracy, you know. What I actually said to Diana that morning was that my intentions were strictly honourable; she seemed content with that.'

Mattie smiled. 'I'm not surprised; I've been rather a trial to her, you know.'

'I can imagine,' Jack acknowledged. 'But I'm quite happy for you to be a trial for me now!'

'In that case, we had better not disappoint my mother, or your family, had we?' Mattie said huskily.

Jack's eyes gleamed darkly. 'Is that a yes to my marriage proposal?'

'Definitely,' she answered with feeling.

How could she do any other than marry Jack? He loved her, she loved him, and both families seemed to approve of their choice. Besides, she quivered all over just at the thought of being Jack's wife, of spending the rest of her life with him.

'You won't regret this, Mattie,' Jack told her fiercely as he pulled her tightly into his arms. 'I'm going to spend the rest of my life loving you,' he promised forcefully.

'And I you,' she vowed.

'That's all that matters,' he accepted before his head lowered and his mouth took possession of hers in a kiss filled with tenderness and love.

It really was all that mattered, Mattie knew inwardly. The future—their future—could take care of itself.

'Do you know, Mattie?' her mother-in-law mused merrily, 'You're the only person I've ever known that's been able to render Jack speechless!' Betty looked at her son as he sat on the other side of Mattie's hospital bed.

Mattie shot her husband a sympathetic look as he sat beside her, their hands tightly linked. 'I have to admit to being a little stunned myself.' She gave a bemused smile, looking past Jack to the two identical cradles that stood at the foot of her bed.

Two babies. Not the one they had been expecting. But twin boys.

Mattie had been as stunned as Jack when, their son newly born and nestled safely in his ecstatic father's arms, her pains had started again, their second son born only two minutes after his brother.

There had been numerous examinations during her pregnancy, several scans, and at no time had anyone suspected that Mattie had carried two babies instead of one.

Mattie, once over the initial surprise, had been absolutely thrilled with their identical sons. Jack, as Betty had just pointed out, was still in shock.

They had been married exactly a year today, the advent of their first child together something they had both looked forward to. As far as Mattie was concerned, her euphoria had only doubled at the appearance of their twin sons.

'What names do you have picked out for them?' Edward Beauchamp asked.

Mattie gave a grateful smile for this change of subject. 'We had chosen James Edward—James for my father,' Mattie explained. 'and Edward for you. But I think— perhaps we'll just settle for James and Edward. What do you think, Jack?' She looked questioningly at her still dazed husband.

'Whatever,' he agreed shakily.

'Betty, perhaps we should just wait outside for a while…?' Edward gave his wife a pointed look. 'Give these two a little time together before Diana and Michael arrive to see their new grandsons.'

They were all one big family now, Diana having married her vet six months ago, the two older couples the best of friends, often having dinner together.

'Yes, of course,' Betty agreed instantly, bending to kiss Mattie warmly on the cheek. 'Edward was just the same when Sally and Cally were born,' she assured Mattie softly. 'He'll get over it.' She looked affectionately at her son. 'It's just the shock.'

Mattie looked searchingly at Jack once they were alone; he didn't really mind that they had two babies instead of the expected one—did he?

'Jack…?' she finally prompted hesitantly.

He looked up at her, fazed. 'I thought—' He swallowed hard. 'It was agony sitting here watching you go through those hours of labour and knowing there was nothing I could do to help you. If I could have had the pain instead of you, I would gladly have done so!' He gave a shuddering sigh. 'Then when the pains started again—! I thought something had gone terribly wrong,' he confided shakily. 'I thought I was going to lose you!' His hand tightened on hers.

Mattie's brow cleared at this further evidence of Jack's love for her. 'I admit, the labour pains weren't pleasant, Jack. But the moment James was born, I forgot about them. And when Edward was born…! Aren't they adorable, Jack?' Her eyes swam with unshed tears as she looked across at their sleeping sons.

Jack stood up to sweep her fiercely into his arms. 'Absolutely adorable,' he agreed. 'Damn it, woman, when are you going to stop surprising me?'

Mattie laughed. 'Never, I hope.'

'So do I.' Jack laughed too, a light sound at the relief of danger having passed. 'I love you, Matilda-May Beauchamp. I always will.'

'I love you too, Jack,' she answered unhesitantly. 'Always.'

Always.

Modern Romance™
...seduction and
passion guaranteed

Tender Romance™
...love affairs that
last a lifetime

Medical Romance™
...medical drama
on the pulse

Historical Romance™
...rich, vivid and
passionate

Sensual Romance™
...sassy, sexy and
seductive

Blaze Romance™
...the temperature's
rising

27 new titles every month.

Live the emotion

MILLS & BOON®

MB3

MILLS & BOON®

Live the emotion

Modern Romance™

THE ITALIAN BOSS'S MISTRESS *by Lynne Graham*

A misunderstanding leads Pippa Stevenson into the bed of her boss, Andreo D'Alessio. The experience is mind-blowing, but afterwards Pippa is covered in shame. And then Andreo decides he wants Pippa all to himself – in the boardroom *and* in the bedroom!

THE BEDROOM SURRENDER *by Emma Darcy*

Adam Cazell lived life in the fast lane – but he stopped dead when he saw Rosalie James. However, a billionaire oozing sex appeal was the last kind of man Rosalie would look at, and spending a week at Adam's island villa with him would be a purely practical arrangement…

A SPANISH VENGEANCE *by Diana Hamilton*

For five years Diego Raffacani has thought of nothing but Lisa – and revenge! Now he's sure she will come to his bed. But he soon realises that he has underestimated the strength of their passion…

THE MILLIONAIRE'S VIRGIN MISTRESS *by Robyn Donald*

Paige Howard has held a secret desire for tycoon Marc Corbett ever since they met. Six years later, she has never felt the same for anyone else. Then, a legacy sends Marc back to Paige, and they are caught again in the grip of their reluctant attraction.

On sale 7th November 2003

Available at most branches of WHSmith, Tesco, Martins, Borders, Eason, Sainsbury's and all good paperback bookshops.

1003/01a

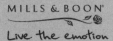

MILLS & BOON®

Live the emotion

Modern Romance™

THE MILLIONAIRE'S MARRIAGE DEMAND by Sandra Field

Julie Renshaw is shocked when Travis Strathern makes an outrageous demand: marriage! Travis is used to getting his own way – but Julie makes certain he won't this time… unless their marriage is based on love as well as passion…

THE GREEK TYCOON'S SECRET CHILD by Cathy Williams

Billionaire Dominic Drecos has sworn off women – until he spots Matilda Hayes! Matilda makes it clear that she is off limits, but Dominic doesn't give up easily. And then the bombshell drops – not only is Dominic her new boss, but she is pregnant with his baby!

CONSTANTINO'S PREGNANT BRIDE by Catherine Spencer

One night of passion had left Cassandra Wilde pregnant with Benedict Constantino's baby – and the Italian tycoon's immediate solution was a marriage of convenience! But, once in Italy, Cassie began to hope their marriage could turn into one of love and passion…

KIDNAPPING HIS BRIDE by Hayley Gardner

Griff Ledoux had always been capable of sweeping Tessa off her feet. And he did it again just as she was about to marry someone else. But could there be anything between them after all these years? And how could Tessa tell him she was only marrying for the sake of his child…?

On sale 7th November 2003

Available at most branches of WHSmith, Tesco, Martins, Borders, Eason, Sainsbury's and all good paperback bookshops.

1003/01b

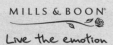
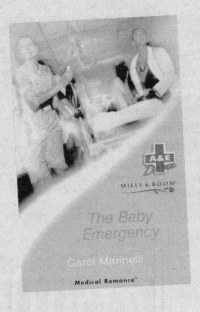